WRATH OF THE CARDINAL

WRATH OF THE CARDINAL
RISE OF THE GRANDMASTER SERIES™ BOOK THREE

BRADFORD BATES
MICHAEL ANDERLE

DISRUPTIVE IMAGINATION

This book is a work of fiction. All of the characters, organizations, and events portrayed in this novel are either products of the author's imagination or are used fictitiously. Sometimes both.

Copyright © 2019 by LMBPN Publishing
Cover Art by Jake @ J Caleb Design
http://jcalebdesign.com / jcalebdesign@gmail.com
Cover copyright © LMBPN Publishing
A Michael Anderle Production

LMBPN Publishing supports the right to free expression and the value of copyright. The purpose of copyright is to encourage writers and artists to produce the creative works that enrich our culture.

The distribution of this book without permission is a theft of the author's intellectual property. If you would like permission to use material from the book (other than for review purposes), please contact support@lmbpn.com. Thank you for your support of the author's rights.

LMBPN Publishing
PMB 196, 2540 South Maryland Pkwy
Las Vegas, NV 89109

Version 1.00, July 2022
Previously published as part of the megabook *Rise Of The Grandmaster*
eBook ISBN: 979-8-88541-707-5
Print ISBN: 979-8-88541-708-2

THE WRATH OF THE CARDINAL TEAM

Thanks to our beta readers
Crystal Wren, Mary Morris, Kelly O'Donnell, John Ashmore, Larry Omans

Thanks to the JIT Readers

Angel LaVey
Billie Leigh Kellar
Dave Hicks
Deb Mader
Diane L. Smith
Dorothy Lloyd
Jackson Hendricks
Jeff Eaton
Jeff Goode
Joshua Ahles
Peter Manis

If I've missed anyone, please let me know!

Editor
The Skyhunter Editing Team

What was the worst that could happen? "The contract I signed to pay for my food and lodging requires me to work. I decided to work with you because I thought learning a skill would be beneficial."

"But why do it at all? None of those bastards at the temple are hurting for gold." Ironbeard poked his head into the front of the shop to make sure no one had wandered in. "Your inn room couldn't possibly cost that much."

Tim smiled. He didn't even know what his inn room would cost if he had to pay for it. "Unlike the temple, I only charge what people can afford for my services. I make a little money, but not the kind you could retire on tomorrow."

The dwarf watched him for a moment, trying to decide if Tim was telling the truth. He seemed to be skeptical about someone not charging an arm and a leg for healing. "Well, I just wanted you to know it's a good thing you're doing. I was actually thinking of giving you some time off every day so you could do more healing."

Ironbeard wagged his finger in Tim's face. "But only if you use the time for healing the needy."

"I might just take you up on that offer." Tim's face grew serious. "I still want to learn more about the work you do here, so I'll promise to use the extra time for healing if you promise to teach me something new every couple of weeks."

"You've got a deal." Ironbeard stuck out his hand.

Tim clasped the dwarf's hand. "So, does this new deal of ours start today?"

The dwarf clapped Tim on the back. "You little shit." He grinned. "Go ahead and get out of here, but if I ever need healing, I expect it to be free of charge."

"Never do anything for free that you can get paid for." Tim laughed at the expression on Ironbeard's face. The dwarf was stuck somewhere between rage and acceptance. "I'm just kidding. If you ever need healing, I'll be happy to do it."

"Good, because I was about to change my mind about letting you go early." He watched Tim as he walked out of the smithy. "Still might if you start slacking off."

Tim left the little shop and headed into the market. He hadn't noticed anyone tracking him since the man with the orange sash died, but it paid to be cautious, especially with Jepsom's representatives making new threats.

Thankfully, he'd taken the lesson his death had taught him to heart. He now carried several different pants and shirt combinations with him. As long as someone didn't see him change clothes, it would be hard for anyone to track him. Tim made his first wardrobe change and continued out of the market.

He thought about using some of his extra time to go and see the high priest, but he really wanted to make it back to the inn. Ernie had found someone who worked in real estate for him to speak to, and Tim wanted to lock up some deals before he made any changes to the slums. If he didn't own the properties, the only people benefitting from the gold he spent would be whoever owned the properties.

Not that the rejuvenation effort was only about making gold, but if someone was going to make gold off of his labor, why shouldn't it be him? The last thing Tim wanted was to make his part of the slums so nice none of the residents could afford to live or work there.

At least most of the buildings near the inn looked like closed commercial properties and not homes. He wouldn't feel like shit for buying an empty building and turning it into something nice. Once he owned a few other properties, he'd get the cobbles put in and place the market kiosk in the inn.

People listing items on the kiosk would save money by not having to travel as far to list them. Hopefully, the money they saved would be spent at the shops lining the street as they left. All he had to do was fix up the buildings and get the right kind of shops in, and he was sitting on a money-generating machine.

If Tim could obtain enough in-game currency, he could afford to send some home to his parents and have enough left over to make a payment on his delayed student loans. Then he could become an adventurer without worrying that he was letting everyone down. Sure he might lose his payment from the company, but if he played his cards right, there was a chance he could make more by taking a risk.

Not exactly a risk when I have five back up plans, Tim thought to himself as he continued walking.

He did wonder if he could keep his job with Ironbeard once he became an adventurer, but he'd worry about that afterward. What he needed to find out now was what the rest of the group wanted. Gaston was an NPC, and he'd been helpful, but they couldn't drag him around forever. The man had to have some kind of life outside of helping them.

Tim was a hundred percent sure ShadowLily was going the adventurer route, and Cassie was probably on board. JaKobi might not be ready to make the decision yet.

Tim would feel a million times better if he knew he would be taking the plunge with a full group already in place.

The only way to find out what everyone wanted was to ask them, something he'd neglected to do for far too long. Some leader he was. All he'd done so far was follow his own agenda, assuming everyone was on board with it. Things had worked out so far, but he had to do better. Friends deserve to feel like they are being included in the group's decision-making, not given orders by the world's worst boss.

Not to mention his girlfriend. There wasn't a woman in the world who would put up with a man who was constantly telling them what to do. At least, he'd never met a man or woman who enjoyed being nagged. ShadowLily was quickly becoming the most important person in his life, and her feelings and desires mattered to him. Tim couldn't say when it had happened, but somewhere along the line, he'd started considering what she would think before he did things.

That was the thing with love. *Once you were in it, you realized that when you made the other person happy, it made you happy.* It was a true partnership when both people in the relationship were selfless. Take care of each other, and everything will turn out fine.

He'd been slacking on his end, and it was time to change that.

Tim smiled as he neared the arch. Two familiar guards were standing in the archway watching something. Last time Tim had seen the guards take an interest in the slums, someone had been stabbed. He didn't get the same vibe right now, so he wondered what was up.

"What do you think those people are doing gathering around the side of the inn?" Chris asked his partner.

"I don't know. Maybe they are trying to guess the airspeed of a swallow." Barry elbowed Chris in the side.

Tim stepped up and peered between them. "Actually, I think they are waiting for me."

"Oh, get a load of this guy, Chris. Thinks he's the duke of the slums," Barry sniggered.

"Duke of the slums." Chris slapped his knee. "That's a good one. I was just going to ask him if he'd started some kind of cult we need to be worried about." Chris looked at Tim. "Anything you'd like to confess?"

"You mean besides the cult I started, and the fact I know how fast a swallow can fly?" Tim stepped between the men before walking under the arch to enter the slums.

"No one knows how fast a swallow flies. That's the whole fucking point!" Barry shouted after him.

"See how he didn't respond to you." Chris poked Barry in the ribs. "Maybe he really *is* duke of the slums."

Tim gazed into the sky as a light rain started to fall. When he'd first entered the game, he'd hated that it always rained on him when he came back to the inn. Now he was starting to like it. The rain let him know he was close to home.

Nothing felt as good as being at home surrounded by the people he cared about.

CHAPTER NINE

"You worthless piece of shit!" Cassie raged.

Tim chuckled as the mug she threw at him was incinerated by JaKobi's flameshield. "If you needed healing, you should have come by the shop."

"I've been hungover and in pain all day." Cassie waved her hand. "Couldn't you have just splashed me with water before you left?"

Tim was pretty sure if he'd splashed her with water while she was passed out, it would have been a lot worse than a thrown mug.

"If I'd known you were hurt, I would have. You two must have crashed right before I left." ShadowLily hadn't come to bed, but Tim had found the two of them draped over the couches downstairs when he had walked out. He looked at ShadowLily, hoping she would help extricate him from the situation.

"Don't look at me." ShadowLily gave Tim a sly smile. "I can't deal with her when she's being dramatic."

Cassie stood up and started pacing back and forth. "Dramatic. Dramatic! I've been stuck by the toilet all day, but lover boy could have fixed it in an instant." She turned and scowled at the healer.

Tim laughed as his healing orb hit Cassie in the face and forced her to stop her tirade. He tried not to gloat because being hungover was the worst. "You were saying?" Tim quickly cast root on her before she could charge him and then followed it up with Cleanse."

"What in the hell was that?" Cassie raged as she wiped off her face.

"Feeling better?" Tim asked hesitantly as he moved toward ShadowLily for protection.

Cassie's glare could have melted the paint off a car. "Maybe, but that was uncalled for."

"Splash me with water. Don't splash me with water. I'm confused now." Tim looked at JaKobi, and the fire mage just shrugged.

ShadowLily gave him a quick kiss. "Go take a bath. You stink."

"Is that what the smell is?" Cassie grinned. "I thought Ernie was making a new concoction."

Tim walked past Cassie on the way to the bathroom and whispered. "You might want to consider taking a bath yourself."

The swift kick to his ass almost sent Tim sprawling. The extra points he'd put into dexterity really saved him from looking like a total fool. He spun around and looked at Cassie's defiant expression before deciding that he was better off accepting the payback for his comment.

He laughed, thinking about Cassie waking up with an inked-on mustache next time he found her passed out on the couch. She reminded him of his little sister, and he'd never let his sister get away with kicking him in the ass. That was the thing with payback; it was a merciless bitch.

Tim was tempted to run back to Cassie so he could mess up

her hair, but he wasn't quite willing to risk it. Instead, he continued to the bathroom. Ah, the hell with it. He couldn't resist taking a parting shot. "If that smell doesn't go away, everyone will know it wasn't just me!"

Dodging the second mug she'd thrown at him in under five minutes, Tim ducked around the corner. A moment later, he popped his head back out, hoping Cassie didn't have another mug in hand. "JaKobi, let the people waiting for healing know I'll be with them soon."

"You got it, boss." The fire mage stood and walked out the entrance.

Tim closed the bathroom door behind him, happy to be alone for a minute. He turned on the water to fill the bath and smiled. Scratch that. His bath would be a million times better if his sexy half-elf seductress was in here with him. There were some activities that were more fun with a partner. Taking a bath was one of them.

Tim walked out of the inn with ShadowLily by his side. She came to help out with security when she didn't have anything better to do. He was lucky to have her since security wasn't a fun job. It normally meant standing around for hours doing absolutely nothing. It was nice to have her and even better for JaKobi, who'd get to spend the afternoon grinding experience to catch up.

Their fire mage was a little behind the curve but moving up quickly. Dude became highly motivated once he found his place after doing bounties with them. If Tim were honest with himself, JaKobi might pass him if he didn't get back to business soon. Between his two jobs and trying to get the slums going, he'd fallen behind his companions. At least he didn't have to worry about his class change quest. Not having to spend a week grinding missions was going to be nice.

JaKobi was leaning against the door of the healing shack. Tim gave him a quick nod and pointed behind him at his girlfriend. "Thanks for keeping an eye on Judy and the shack, but ShadowLily decided to give you the afternoon off."

JaKobi stepped in front of Tim before he could enter. "You might want me to stay for a few minutes when you see who's inside."

Doubt started to burrow through his mind. "Another of Jepsom's men?"

Before the fire mage could answer, ShadowLily cut him off. "You didn't tell me the cardinal sent someone here. How are we going to keep you safe if you don't give us all the details?"

Tim looked at JaKobi and quickly realized he wasn't going to get any help from him. He turned back toward ShadowLily and smiled sheepishly. "It slipped my mind."

"Weak." ShadowLily pulled Tim close. "I don't want you dying on me, so you have to tell me what kind of trouble you're getting into."

JaKobi smiled at the two of them. They were on the border of being so cute he wanted to gag, but secretly he hoped to have the same kind of relationship one day. "The trouble seems to be of the half-orc variety."

Tim's face went pale. "Malvonis is here?"

"Didn't give me a name." JaKobi shrugged. "Just showed me a big knife and said he'd be waiting inside."

"Where's Judy?" Tim looked around, hoping to see her outside.

JaKobi worked his mouth like he was sucking on something sour. "She said not to worry about her, that she had work to do." He made air quotes. "I'm not leaving because some asshole with a knife wants to harass the boss."

Turning away from the mage, Tim looked at ShadowLily. "Go get Cassie and Gaston, but stay outside until I call for you." He turned to face the door and nodded to JaKobi. "You're with me."

"You got it, boss." The fire mage stepped forward and pushed open the door.

Tim walked into the shack first and was pleasantly surprised not to see Judy cut to ribbons. Malvonis was sitting in a chair by the wall, eating something that looked suspiciously like grapes. He had a smile on his face that made his tusks stick out a bit farther than normal.

Judy had finished getting the towels and the water ready and was about to step outside. "Tell your friend he'd better be picking up his own damn seeds."

Tim looked at her stern face and the pits on the ground. "JaKobi, do you mind?"

The fire mage lifted one eyebrow in question, and when Tim gave him a subtle nod, he started casting a spell. With one wave of his hand, the scattered seeds on the floor burst into flame. All that was left of them were tiny wisps of smoke.

Tim watched Malvonis but didn't see any hint of surprise, although he was pretty sure JaKobi's spell got the message across. The half-orc now knew Tim had a fire mage on his side who was good enough to incinerate several targets at once. The message also said, don't fuck with my place, or you might be next.

"Judy, I'm going to have a word with our guest. When you see him leave, send in the first client."

"Of course, sir." Judy flashed Tim a brief smile, scowled at Malvonis, and closed the door.

Malvonis stood up from the chair and tucked the remaining grapes inside his cloak. "You've got a nice little racket going on here, but the cardinal wants it to stop."

"So Jepsom sent you after his man failed to get the answer he wanted?" Tim moved to stand in front of the sitting thief. "I thought we had an understanding about you not coming back here?"

"When I took the job, I didn't know I'd be coming back here." Malvonis gave Tim a sly smile. "Can't we just make this easy on each other? The message from the cardinal is simple: Stop healing, or things will get worse."

A ball of flame appeared in JaKobi's hand. "Is that a threat?"

"Call it a friendly suggestion." Malvonis shrugged his massive shoulders. "If this situation was going to come to violence, I wouldn't have announced myself. I find that killing goes much easier when the person you are trying to murder doesn't expect it."

Tim held up his hand to silence JaKobi's reply. "Consider your message delivered. Kindly tell the cardinal I'm not interested in his offer."

The half-orc's smile disappeared. "He won't be pleased with your answer."

"Then he can take it up with the high priest, whose blessing I have." Tim was starting to get worked up, but he'd be damned if he was going to be the first one to lose his temper. "I actually needed to see him, so I'll just fill him in on Jepsom's messengers in the morning."

Malvonis held up his hands in front of him in a slow the fuck down gesture. "Seems as though I've found myself in the middle of a political squabble I'd rather not be a part of. Being on the bad side of either of those men isn't good for your health. Despite what you might think about my profession as a whole, it's much safer than playing politics."

"Tell me about it," Tim groused as he thought of everything he'd done in the game so far. All of it, every little thing he'd been through, was because of Cardinal Jepsom's ambition. "I'd much rather the two of them worked this out themselves, so I could stop looking over my shoulder for who was going to try to kill me next."

"Not going to happen any time soon," Malvonis grumbled. "I don't know what you did to piss that guy off, but he's got a real hard-on for you now."

Tim shook his head in disgust. His life would be so much easier if Jepsom simply disappeared. "I get the feeling the cardinal's support inside the temple is waning. Might be a good time to pick the other side."

If Tim could get Malvonis out of the picture, his life would sure as hell be a lot simpler. Shit, if he could get him to fight for the high priest instead, he might not even have to fight with Jepsom himself. In a perfect world, he'd be able to orchestrate the whole thing, but inside *The Etheric Coast*, he didn't have that kind of pull.

"I don't pick sides. The only thing I do is take a job and see it through to the end. If coming down here and roughing you up gets me square with that evil bastard, I'll do it." Malvonis eyed Tim, making sure his hand didn't stray toward his dagger. "But I'm just as inclined to call it a day as long as you help me out."

JaKobi extinguished the fireball he'd been holding. "Why would you do that?"

Malvonis shook his head, clearly asking himself the same question. "Normally, I wouldn't, but the cardinal just wanted the message delivered. He doesn't want you dead." He scratched absentmindedly at a scar on his arm. "At least not yet."

Looking around the shack, the half-orc started to smile. "People working for the cardinal have a way of disappearing. I'm not keen on joining their ranks."

"I might have disappeared a few of them." Tim wondered if he'd said too much. "But I'm sure the cardinal is much more efficient at it than I am."

The half-orc started walking toward the door. "As long as you're okay putting on a show, I'll just leave. After I tell the cardinal I've roughed you up, I think I'll take a vacation until the rest of the temple's drama is sorted out."

Tim looked at JaKobi. "Tell the others to stand down."

Grinning, Malvonis stepped out of the way so the fire mage could leave the room. "You had people ready in case I attacked. Smart, very smart." His tusks jutted out when the half-orc's mouth opened in a grin. "I think I'm starting to like you, kid."

"I don't like taking chances." Tim looked at the half-orc, and despite Malvonis' change in tactics, there was no way he could trust this man not to come back and kill him if the cardinal asked him too.

Anything Tim said to the thief right now might as well be said straight to the cardinal. "So, what's your plan?"

Malvonis grabbed one of the pots full of water. Turning away from Tim, he kicked open the door and stormed out. Before walking down the steps, he threw the pot back inside, where it shattered, splashing water everywhere. "And don't you forget what I fucking told you!"

The half-orc pulled up his hood and stalked toward the exit of the slums. Tim watched him go, wondering just how much trouble he was in. If the cardinal sent Malvonis to kill him in the future, there was a good chance he'd end up dead. Getting to level ten and becoming an adventurer was looking more appealing by the second.

Tim pondered his options, realizing there was really just one question he needed to ask. How long would it be before the cardinal took the next step? He had to see Paul and find out what it was going to take to end this. Tim had finally reached the end of his rope with that bastard. Jepsom's threats had to stop; he had more important things to worry about. It was time to turn the tables and let the cardinal find out what it felt like to be powerless.

Judy looked into the healing shack to make sure nothing else had been destroyed and started cleaning up the mess. He made a mental note to give his assistant a hearty bonus at the end of the night.

Turning away from the mess, he looked at the members of his guild. "We'll talk as soon as I finish healing these folks."

"That's fine, but none of us are going anywhere." ShadowLily frowned at Malvonis' back as he slowly continued on his way to the arch.

"I knew there was a reason I kept you around." Tim kissed ShadowLily on the lips.

"I was thinking it was because of the great sex and my sparkling personality, but now we've gotten to the truth of the matter. You just like my knives." The half-elven thief pulled out her blades and spun them on her palms.

"As long as you aren't throwing them at me." Tim immediately thought about the time he'd had a teacup on his head. He'd never be dumb enough to make that bet again.

"You two make me wanna barf." Cassie chuckled. "Now that the drama alert is over, I'm going to finish my bath. Scream really loud if you need me before then."

Tim smiled at the thought of a naked Cassie jumping out of one of the windows with her staff in hand, ready to save them all. If that ever happened, he'd have to get her picture put on a coffee mug.

Gaston ignored their byplay, focusing his attention on JaKobi. "Do you know how to play Kill the King?" He wrapped an arm around the man's shoulders and started leading him to a little table set up outside of the door. "Why don't I show you?"

If JaKobi was smart, he'd keep his coins in his pouch. Rule one was to never play cards with Gaston if you wanted to leave with any of your gold.

Tim looked at the gathered faces and said to the first person in line. "I'm sorry for the delay, ma'am. Please come inside, and I'll get you fixed right up."

Judy helped the older woman up the three stairs and into the shack. This was what it was all about. He was a healer, and these people needed him. There was no way he would stop when they deserved a fighting chance to thrive. Like a flower growing in the cracks of a sidewalk, life would find a way.

His job was to make that life a little more bearable.

CHAPTER TEN

"I need a beer," Tim called as he entered the inn.

Ernie smiled at the young healer. "And some food, if I'm not mistaken."

Liz came out of the kitchen carrying a tray covered in bowls with little silver lids and loaves of hard, crusty bread. Another night of stew. Tim grimaced. But hey, at least the food had gotten better since Liz started. Not that she did the cooking, but she was helping Ernie vet new cooks to take over the kitchen.

To be fair, the reason the chefs were making so much stew was because she wanted to create a baseline to judge them by. If they all cooked different meals, how people voted might depend on the person or the day. Now they'd had one meal from each of the cooks, and the guild could put in their votes for who they liked best.

Each dish seemed better than the last to Tim, but he was getting sick of stew. He might love a bowl of the stuff, especially on a cold and rainy night, but not for every dinner for two weeks in a row.

It was a little much.

The bowl in front of him smelled divine. It was the first time someone had made more of a cream base than a traditional stew. He felt like he was eating a steak version of chicken and dumplings with potatoes instead of dumplings.

That was the thing with food, Tim might not be able to cook it or to describe it very well, but he sure as hell knew how to eat it. He ripped off the heel of the bread and dipped it into his bowl. When it had soaked up enough of the sauce, he ate it ravenously.

Tim looked up after finishing his bread and noticed that everyone else in the room was watching him. "What?" he mumbled as he ripped off another chunk from the loaf.

"We've all been waiting to find out what in the fuck Malvonis wanted, and you haven't even looked at us." ShadowLily sat next to him. "So, what's up?"

Tim set down his bread and covered the bowl of stew with the lid, knowing full well by the time they were done talking, his dinner wouldn't be hot anymore. "Jepsom sent him to tell me to stop healing people outside the temple."

Taking a sip of beer to clear his throat, Tim continued, "Malvonis was annoyed when he found out the high priest and Jepsom weren't on the same page when it came to my healing. I'd say he left because he wanted to avoid pissing off Paul, but I don't think the bastard does anything unless he wants to. That means we probably haven't seen the last of him."

Tim polished off his beer and motioned for Liz to bring him another one. "On the plus side, if we end up in a confrontation with the cardinal and have to take him out, our potential Malvonis issue disappears." Tim looked around the table at the shocked faces. "Just saying."

"Makes sense to me. Why fight when you can get two of your enemies to wipe each other out?" JaKobi tapped a finger on his chin in thought. "It's kind of brilliant, really. Like when the Sith use the trade federation to get shit done."

"You know, not everything can be tied back to a *Star Wars* movie plot." Cassie glared at the fire mage.

"Just try me," JaKobi fired back, grinning ear from ear.

Tim smiled at the fire mage. He couldn't help it. JaKobi's love of all things *Star Wars* was infectious. He was just about to try to trip him up when ShadowLily elbowed him in the ribs.

"Let's not get off-track," ShadowLily looked at the two of them. "What we decide to do next is important."

"Speaking of important." Tim deflected answering whatever her next question was going to be by asking one of his own. "I've been meaning to find out what everyone's plans are after they hit level ten and complete their class change quests."

"Maybe we should worry about the super-assassin the cardinal hired to rough you up." Cassie looked at Tim incredulously. "Priorities, man, priorities."

"Not much I can do until I go see the high priest. I'm not sure the five of us are strong enough to take out the cardinal even if we wanted to, not that I would even try without Paul's blessing."

JaKobi snorted. "Too bad Jepsom doesn't feel the same way about taking you out."

"Tell me about it," Cassie grumbled.

"You should see the high priest tomorrow." ShadowLily looked at Tim, her face etched with concern. She put one finger over his lips before he could speak. "Before work."

"I was afraid you were going to say that." Tim groaned. "I'm going to take the rest of this food up to my room and get ready for bed." He mock-glared at his girlfriend. "Apparently, I have an early-morning appointment."

"There are some perks to going to bed early." ShadowLily picked up her own bowl and headed for the stairs. "I'll see you up there."

Tim knew she was being flirty to try to keep his mind off what might happen tomorrow. Going to see Paul wasn't without risk. He'd already been banned from practicing at the temple for defying Jepsom's orders. Going back inside might mean his death if the wrong people found him before he made it to the high priest.

He started walking toward the stairs but paused and turned to face the members of his guild. "Remember to think about what you want out of your time in the game. I want whatever we do next to benefit all of us."

JaKobi nodded. "You've got it, boss."

"I'm already doing what I want. The only thing that would make it better is more money." Cassie smiled. "You've really gotta quit your job so we can do bounties during the day."

"That would be kinda awesome." JaKobi smiled, thinking about all the loot they could earn.

"So, you both want to be adventurers?" Tim thought about how easily they'd made the choice and how hard he was struggling with his.

"You don't?" Cassie asked in disbelief.

Tim almost laughed at the look of shock on her face. "I didn't say that. It's just that I need to have a few things in place before I can take the leap."

Cassie huffed. "Better get on it. We're all waiting on you."

Tapping his spoon on the lid covering his soup, Tim sighed. "You're going to have to wait a little longer—and don't make that face. We've done tons of cool stuff so far."

"Yeah, but think about all the stuff we're missing out on while you're at work." She elbowed JaKobi in an attempt to get him to agree with her. "Right?"

The fire mage grinned. "Yes, we've done lots of cool stuff."

"Pussy," Cassie said as she poked JaKobi in the ribs hard enough to make him grunt before she turned her attention back to Tim. "Seriously, think of all the stuff we could do if you didn't have to work."

Tim had come into the game with a plan. He was here to

make enough gold to send some real-world currency home to his family and pay off his student loans. Until Tim knew he could accomplish those feats as an adventurer, he had to keep his options open.

It felt like he was being pulled in one direction, and he had no idea if the game was manipulating him into becoming an adventurer or if it was something he truly wanted. Tim felt alive when they were out running bounties and conquering dungeons, but he couldn't let that excitement overrun his pragmatism. Sometimes you had to stick with boring and reliable.

But you also had to be willing to risk it all if you wanted to succeed.

Was he willing to put his future on the line by dedicating all of his time in-game to making more money, or was he going to stick with the basics and come out with a guaranteed payout? It was hard to put all your effort into a dream that might not pay out in the end.

But he wanted to be an adventurer badly enough to dedicate himself to his dream completely.

The hardest part for him was knowing that he was doing it for the right reasons. He didn't want the fame that followed some of the gamers when they finally called it quits. Tim only wanted this to work because of what it could mean for his future.

Gaming was something he loved, and making money at it would be the ultimate job. Working together with a team to take down the biggest baddies in the game was something he lived for when he was behind the screen. Now that he was on the screen, did he really expect those feelings to be different?

Part of him was dead-set on staying firm and doing the job he'd been assigned, but the other part of him, the part that fed his imagination, was already setting things up. Tim's work in the slums wasn't bringing in any money yet, but it would, and with a safety net in place, he felt a lot better about making the switch from worker to adventurer.

Tim smiled as he realized he'd become lost in his thoughts while JaKobi and Cassie were waiting for an answer to her question. He decided to play it off for now and mark them down for a more serious discussion later. "You know me. I've got to plan things out before I make a decision."

"By 'plan,' he means shout out orders and pray that everything doesn't turn to shit in an instant," Cassie said drolly to JaKobi.

"Whatever Tim's doing seems to be working. I'm more concerned about these guys from the temple showing up and trying to take us out."

"Well, there is always something to look forward to." Tim turned away from his friends and walked up the stairs.

Cassie shouted after him, "We have very different ideas about what to get excited about."

"I don't know. If I was heading upstairs to ShadowLily, I'd be excited too." JaKobi said with a smile.

Cassie elbowed him in the ribs. "Don't be gross. Save that shit for your guy friends."

The fire mage held up his hands in surrender. "I was talking to Gaston."

The assassin picked up his soup and left the room without saying a word. Ernie and Liz followed him out, leaving JaKobi sitting alone with Cassie. "Isn't this soup delicious?" he stammered.

Tim smiled at himself as he watched the two of them from the landing on the stairs. Once he realized Cassie wasn't going to pick a fight, he continued up the stairs to his room. The Guild was becoming more than a group of adventurers. They might even be more than just friends.

To Tim, the guild members already felt like family.

CHAPTER ELEVEN

The streets of Promethia were almost empty this early in the morning.

Tim thought about the traffic around campus in the morning and realized he didn't miss it at all. There was something to be said about some good old fashioned peace and quiet. Not to mention the lack of cars. The air seemed to smell sweeter, but that could just be the game enhancing his experience.

Walking to the temple wouldn't take too long, and it felt much better doing it with boots on. His first day in the game, Tim had made the trek without shoes, and he was happy he'd never have to do that again. Who would have thought finding footwear was such a big deal?

He slowed down as he came to a spot where he could look between the buildings toward the market and the warehouses. Peeking out behind the large structures was the harbor and the docks that helped make this city flourish. Men and women were already working hard on the docks and in the market. They moved like ants swarming over a piece of fallen fruit, setting up stalls, displaying their wares, and loading and unloading boxes from the ships.

The market was the one place that was truly alive all day long. The workers and the shoppers might change, but it was always busy. It was exactly the same kind of environment he wanted to create in the slums. Why shouldn't there be somewhere else to shop?

Especially when the gold that shopping brought in went straight into his pockets.

His stomach did a little flip as the temple steps came into view. It wasn't easy to walk headfirst into what might be a trap, but Tim had to speak to Paul. Thankfully there were people making their way inside for healing or prayer already. Tim hoped he could slip in with the crowd and then find one of the acolytes to take him to the high priest. He might be able to find Paul's chambers on his own, but there was a better chance that he'd end up lost for hours in the temple's winding halls.

Tim ducked his head down as he started up the steps. Jepsom didn't have as many followers as he used to, but he still had eyes and ears all over the temple. He joined the others in line and continued shuffling up the steps until they reached the temple doors.

The inside of the entrance was just as grand as Tim remembered from his first trip. Pillars held up a vaulted ceiling; the place felt as if the roof were in the heavens themselves. It still mystified him to this day how men could use stone in such a way. There was a certain amount of craftsmanship slowly lost in the real world.

When was the last time someone built something that truly inspired people? Tim would have loved to see the look on people's faces when the churches and chapels were built in the middle ages. Imagine coming from a village where you still had thatched roofs and seeing something like the Sistine Chapel or the Notre Dame Cathedral.

It would have been life-changing.

Kind of like deciding to enter *The Etheric Coast* was for Tim. Outside of the game, he would have been stuck in an office crunching numbers and hoping to make a wealthy client even wealthier. Here he was leading the fight against a usurper inside the temple and trying to build something from scratch.

There was something to be said about living in a world where the only thing holding you back was your desire to be successful. Inside the game, people were still completing world firsts. There was a whole new land of opportunities to explore here. Things that no other person had discovered were waiting to be found.

Promethia was literally brand new.

Tim thought about how connected they were back in the real world. You could get in touch with anyone at any time from anywhere in the world. It was nuts, and yet people still seemed to spend more time alone.

Come into *The Etheric Coast*, and you could only send in-game messages that might as well have been physical letters to other players. If you wanted to talk to an NPC, you had to get off your lazy ass and go find them. And for Tim, sending in-game messages kind of broke his immersion. Now that ShadowLily was with him almost all the time, he didn't check his messages as often as he should.

This was his home now, and he would be here for a long time. Whatever he had to do to make the game feel real, he was going to do it. Tim felt like he was LARPing at a Renaissance festival. Only when he went home, he didn't have to get ready for school in the morning.

Now that Tim was well inside the temple, he started to look for one of the younger members the church used for runners. He spotted one across the room and made his way to the boy. The kid, dressed in a simple brown smock, was standing off to the side, waiting to be called to task by one of the brothers.

Plastering a confused smile on his face, Tim approached the boy. "Excuse me, good sir. I was wondering if you could help me?"

The boy looked shocked at being addressed directly. "I can escort you to one of the brothers if you need assistance."

"I do so hate to be a bother." Tim kept his smile in place as he looked around the temple. "It's just that the high priest asked me to meet him here, and I have no idea how to find his chambers."

Now the kid looked slightly panicked. "The high priest?"

"Yes, do you think you can help me track him down?" Tim tried to put just the right note of hopefulness in his voice.

"I can find one of the brothers to escort you." The boy started to turn away from Tim.

"That won't do at all." Tim stopped the boy from turning and slipped a gold coin into his hand. "Let's not waste a brother's time with this. If we get there and he doesn't wish to see me, surely his guards will turn me away at the door."

"I don't know if I should," the kid stammered.

Tim looked directly into the boy's eyes. "I promise you that I have an appointment, and he will be happy to see me." He looked from side to side and lowered his voice to a conspiratorial whisper. "But there are others here who might not be as excited by my intrusion."

The acolyte thought about it for a moment, then reached out to grab Tim's hand. "Follow me." The kid was wearing a look that said it wouldn't be his fault if the guards tossed the man out on his ass.

It took the kid about fifteen minutes to get Tim in front of the giant golden door of the high priest's chambers. They'd passed a number of brothers in the hallway. A few of them stared at them curiously, but none tried to stop them. A few times, he'd held his breath, waiting to be stabbed in the back by one of Jepsom's men, but the attack never came.

The golden door started to swing open, and Tim looked at the boy. "Thanks for your help."

He watched as the kid ran off without saying a word. Maybe he had better places to be, but Tim got the feeling the runner he'd sequestered didn't want to be seen here, at least not with him. With the door open, he walked forward. There was no reason to stand on ceremony. It was time to find out what Paul had in store for him.

The high priest stepped down from his simple wooden throne and walked toward Tim with his hand extended. "I'm happy to see you. When you didn't show up right after Lady Briarthorn's party, I was worried something might have happened to you."

Tim shook Paul's hand. "It's good to see you." He let go and made sure to look the man straight in the eyes. "Nothing has happened to me yet, but Cardinal Jepsom has sent a couple of men down to the slums to stop me from healing."

One of Paul's eyes twitched, and his cheeks turned red. "He *what?*"

"He sent some priest named Dunstin to see me, and when I told him to fuck off, he sent Malvonis." Tim felt the fury coming off of Paul in waves and thought he'd better de-escalate the situation. "But we were able to handle it."

"Sending a brother is one thing, but retaining outside help is something else entirely." Paul turned away from Tim, walked back to his throne, and sat down. "Apparently our efforts to stop the cardinal have only made him bolder."

The high priest let out a heavy sigh. "I hoped removing his top three associates from the temple would be a firm enough reminder of who was in charge, but it seems he has taken my actions as just another slap on the wrist."

Paul shook his head in disgust. "I believed there was still a way to return Cardinal Jepsom to the goddess' light. He was a good man once, not that you could tell by looking at him today.

Something has to be done about him," Paul said as he wrung his hands with worry.

Tim wondered if this was going to be the moment he finally got the kill quest. There was no doubt in his mind that destroying Jepsom was the final step in this chain. Every single thing he'd done had brought him closer to this moment. All he needed was for Paul to say the word.

"What do you need me to do?" Tim watched the high priest, his anticipation making him twitchy.

"I think it's time we ended this. Cardinal Jepsom's time amongst the living must be brought to an end. May the goddess have mercy on his soul."

Quest Received: Wrath of the goddess

It's time for you to end Cardinal Jepsom's time on this plane, but it can't be done inside the temple. Paul has scheduled an event to honor the cardinal. It will be held in seven days, and you will be given a copy of the itinerary.

Your reward will be determined by the results.

Accept Quest: Yes/No

Tim quickly accepted the quest.

Paul stood up and extended his hand. "The goddess thanks you." Paul pulled a book that had a faint golden glow around it from his robes. "Her appreciation isn't without benefits." He handed the book to Tim.

The leather binding was hand-stitched, and the golden glow had to be coming from some kind of magic infused into the book. Tim wasn't sure what he was being handed. It could have been a bible, or maybe a weapon for his off hand. He accepted the book and reviewed the flowing script on the cover, which read *Healing Storm*. Was this a spell book?

Thinking back to his first day in the game, Tim opened it. Power seemed to flow through him and he was lifted into the air. When his feet touched the ground a moment later, he knew the spell completely. A prompt appeared in his vision.

Skill Granted: Healing Storm
Rank: Novice Level One
The Goddess Eternia once pointed her hand toward the heavens and bathed an entire city in holy rain. You might not be able to heal a city yet, but a group of five players shouldn't be a problem.
Healing Storm is an AOE (Area of Effect) spell that can heal up to five party members as long as they are standing within the spell's radius.

It was his first AOE spell. As long as everyone crowded together, he could heal all of them with one spell. The mana cost might hurt after a bit, but it saved Tim the trouble of casting separate healing orbs on each person. It would be a real lifesaver, especially in a situation where everyone was taking damage at the same time.

If Tim was able to level the spell up enough, he might even be able to heal through some of the boss' status effects. No more jumping into the river to get rid of the acid. Just keep killing, and he'd be able to keep you alive.

That was his job, after all.

"Paul, this is more than I deserve," Tim mumbled, still not quite believing his luck.

The high priest shook his head from side to side. "For all that you've done in service of the goddess, you deserve it. I trust that when the time comes to carry out this last task, you won't hesitate?"

Tim had to think about it for a moment. He'd waffled about the killing thing for too long. This was a game, and he was a hero. Stamping out evil wherever he found it was part of every hero's journey. No one ever shouted, "Hey that Lancelot is a real looker, too bad he's shit with a sword." One of the biggest parts of being a hero was the ability to take down the game's most vile enemies.

Jepsom certainly counted as vile.

He wondered why it had taken him so long to come to grips with killing the NPCs. It probably had something to do with the NPCs in this game feeling so real. It wasn't like he could walk through his neighborhood back home and smite people for bad attitudes or not trimming their grass.

He'd leave the grass-measuring homicides to Dennis Rader.

Here in *The Etheric Coast*, the people felt just as real as the ones back home, but they weren't. He didn't have to feel bad about killing an NPC as long as he was on the right side of things. It also helped that Jepsom was a giant ass. He might have a problem killing an innocent man, but the cardinal was anything but innocent.

Tim looked into Paul's searching eyes and spoke with resolve. "You can count on me to handle it. I won't let you down."

"May the goddess' light shine upon you," Paul intoned. "I'll do my best to spread the word to our people that they are not to interfere with any healing taking place in the slums. Mentioning that the healer working there has been blessed by the goddess herself and is to be left alone should be a sufficient story to accomplish that goal."

Shaking the high priest's hand again, Tim couldn't help but grin. This was really going to piss Jepsom off, and angry people made mistakes. "Thank you so much, Paul. I'll have to get with my team, but I think we might be able to handle this quickly."

"Then go into the world and spread the light of the goddess to those who need it most." Paul made the sign of the goddess over his chest and called for one of his guards to lead Tim out of the temple.

Tim looked back once to see Paul sitting on his throne, head bowed in thought or prayer. It couldn't have been easy to condemn one of his own to death, but sometimes you had to cut out the rot before the infection could spread. Hopefully, having the blessing of the goddess eased the high priest's mind.

Tim stepped into the sunshine and felt a sense of determination. This part of his journey was almost over. After he finished his quest for the temple, he'd be able to move onto something else. Maybe they could find a new dungeon to explore, or another quest chain meant for a group instead of just him.

Whatever the future held, Tim had the feeling it would be fucking awesome.

CHAPTER TWELVE

"Come on. Let's go," Cassie whined.

"But Tim should be back in a couple hours, and I want to know what happened at the temple." ShadowLily leaned back in her chair and propped her feet up. She hoped Cassie would get the point.

"That's why we have to go now." Cassie put her hands on her hips. "You know as well as I do that as soon as lover boy gets back, we're going to get roped into some crazy scheme."

ShadowLily grinned at her best friend. "I do know. Why do you think I'm trying to rest right now?"

Cassie kicked ShadowLily's feet off the chair and sat across from her. "If we leave now, I'm sure we'll be back before he gets here." She knew no such thing, but getting the last step of her class change quest done was too important for whole truths.

"Do you really think we'll be back in time?" ShadowLily's expression said she hoped what Cassie said was true, but she was also just really tired of sitting around.

"Of course, we will. Remember how quick the last part of your class change quest was." Cassie smiled reassuringly. "We got this."

"Fine." ShadowLily turned away from her wily little friend and looked at the fire mage. "JaKobi, can you handle guard duty later?"

He looked at the book he was reading. "I don't know. My schedule's kind of full." He held up the book to make sure she saw it.

"I hope that's a joke." ShadowLily stood up and walked toward him. "What are you reading, anyway?"

"*History of Ragnus the Burner.* Apparently, he was a grandmaster fire mage who snapped and started burning people alive as sacrifices to the Shining God." He set the book down. "And yes, it was a joke. I don't mind staying with Tim while you knock out Cassie's quest."

Cassie blew a raspberry at JaKobi from across the room. "Don't pout because I didn't ask you to come."

"Don't worry. You can pay me back by helping with my class change." The fire mage beamed at her affectionately.

Cassie stood up and grabbed her bō staff from where it rested against the table. "See, Tim's in good hands. Let's go do this thing."

ShadowLily tapped her fingers on the back cover of JaKobi's book. "Do you think there is more than one God in the game right now?"

"There could be, but this is from at least five hundred years ago." JaKobi laughed at Cassie's exaggerated hurry the fuck up expression. "When we have some time, I can talk to one of the mages in the great library. I'm sure they would know if the people of *The Etheric Coast* worship multiple members of the divine."

"What does it matter?" Cassie whined. "Let's get a move on. We don't want to be late for lover boy's triumphant return."

"It matters because if there is more than one god, there could be repercussions for helping one of them." ShadowLily frowned. "I've never read a story where there were multiple gods who lived amongst each other in harmony."

"But that wouldn't have anything to do with us." Cassie motioned toward the door. When ShadowLily didn't move, she grabbed her hand and started pulling.

"Says the lady resurrected by the goddess." ShadowLily let Cassie drag her toward the door. "JaKobi, if you think you can make it back on time, I'd love to find out the answer."

The fire mage grinned as he watched ShadowLily struggle in the doorway, waiting for his answer. He'd never felt as important as he did right now. Having someone wait on your very words felt oddly satisfying to him. "I'll follow you out." JaKobi tucked the book back into his inventory and headed for the door.

ShadowLily gave him a wave and let Cassie pull her outside.

"I thought you said this would be easy," ShadowLily wheezed out between gasps.

"It was easy until they started chasing us." Cassie grinned like Nicholas Cage in *Face Off*. "But we've got this."

ShadowLily jumped over a fallen log and picked up her pace. "Tell me again how we got this?"

"You're acting like it's my fault. How was I supposed to know the cool-ass jungle hidden inside a cave would be filled with giant lizard-men? This isn't my fault; the quest is marked solo. Why would I plan on running into a shit-ton of monsters? All I did was follow the quest arrow on my map." A branch hit Cassie in the face and scratched her below the eye.

Cassie wiped the blood away but kept running. "Never a healer around when you need one."

"We could have had one, but you didn't want to wait," ShadowLily snapped.

A group of lizard-men with shields and swords appeared on their left, forcing the two women to turn right and keep running. Cassie got the distinct impression they were being funneled farther into the jungle when all they wanted to do was leave and come back with a full group. She looked behind her one more time to confirm they were still being chased.

Cassie's grin disappeared. She was pretty sure the lizard-men could have run them down by now if they truly wanted to. The bastards had to be seven or eight feet tall. The lizard-men also had huge tails that they used like third legs to run even faster. While Cassie considered herself pretty fast, this was like Michael Phelps trying to outswim a Great White; it was never going to happen.

Not to mention, if the fuckers weren't trying to catch them, they might be in real trouble.

She kept running though because facing off against fifteen of the giant green-skinned monsters with just the two of them was suicide. Cassie hadn't completed her class change quest yet, and she was pretty sure the goddess was done handing out favors. It must be tough being a goddess. The number of people constantly hounding you for help had to be overwhelming.

What Cassie wanted right now was a get the hell out of Dodge. If this was Monopoly, the lizard-men wouldn't be allowed past go, but this wasn't a board game. There was no way to know what would happen if they were caught, although she doubted it would be pleasant. Instead of hoping things would work out for the best, Cassie pushed her legs to move a little faster. Eventually, she'd run out of endurance, but she wasn't going to give up.

Giving up just wasn't in her.

Cassie had spent most of her life being told she was too small. Sure it came in handy when they wanted her to be on top of the pyramid or to stand in front for a photo, but it sucked when they were picking teams. It didn't matter that she could drop dimes on the basketball court or kick the shit out of a soccer ball. People saw her and thought, "She's too small to be good."

She didn't let the haters bring her down in the real world, and she sure as hell wasn't going to let some overaggressive lizards do it to her now. When the moment they were too tired to keep running came, she'd turn and fight. Those green fuckers wouldn't know what hit them.

ShadowLily was already starting to slow. Her higher dexterity was nice for fights when she needed to dodge and get stabby, but for cross-country marathons, it wasn't the stat she needed.

It was almost time to make the choice. If she had to decide between getting shot in the back by arrows or hacked apart by swords while running away, she'd rather go down swinging. Cassie glanced at her friend, hoping she wouldn't be the cause of ShadowLily's first death after becoming an adventurer.

"I don't know about you, but I've done about all the running I can." Cassie lunged to the left to avoid a branch, but quickly corrected her course as another group of lizard-men appeared out of thin air to keep them on track.

Cassie couldn't shake the feeling that they were being herded toward something.

ShadowLily tried to smile, but her chest was heaving so hard, it looked more like a grimace. "I'm not missing the heals as much as I'm missing Tim's ideas. I could really go for one of his crazy plans right now."

"Me too." Cassie gulped for air. "But if you tell him I said that, I'll have to kill you."

"Might not be alive long enough for you to get the chance." ShadowLily pointed at a giant hole in front of them.

"Fuck!" Cassie screamed as she skidded to a stop.

There wasn't anywhere for them to go. Lizard-men stepped out of the dense foliage, creating a path that led to only one place: the fucking hole. The giant fuckers who had been chasing them filled the gaps between trees. They raised their shields and slowly marched forward. Cassie felt like she was in the movie *300* and was about to get kicked into the well.

If she was going to die, it'd be on her terms.

"You should stealth and see if you can get out of here," Cassie whispered as she pulled her staff from behind her back. She'd been playing around with her new trident, but the weight of the tip threw off her movements. For now, she was sticking with her old tried and true bō staff.

"And let you have all the fun?" ShadowLily's bravado might have been faked, but it sure as fuck made Cassie feel better.

"This is Sparta!" Cassie roared and charged toward the line of shields.

Her bō staff clanged harmlessly off the solid iron shields. Despite Cassie's best efforts, she couldn't land a single hit against the well-organized lizard-men. They snarled fiercely as they used their shields to push them toward the precipice. It reminded her of riot police trying to clear a street.

There was only one place the two of them were going.

ShadowLily tried to dart through a gap in the shields, but it closed quickly, and she was slammed in the chest by one of the shields. The lizard-men waited for her to stand up before herding them toward the hole again.

"You know, the Spartans kicked their enemies into the well, right?" ShadowLily tried to smile, but her eyes had the look of a trapped animal.

"They also had abs of steel," Cassie retorted.

ShadowLily took a step back. The lip of the hole was only twenty feet away now. "What in the fuck do their abs have to do with anything?"

"If I'm going to die, I want to do it thinking about being surrounded by three hundred men whose abs I could scrub my clothes on."

"Gerard Butler, I've got a new role for you to consider." ShadowLily grinned. "It's playing a washboard in a film titled *Cassie Does Laundry.*"

"I'd fucking watch the shit out of that." Cassie looked over the edge of the pit as they shuffled backward. It wouldn't be long now before they had to put up or shut up.

"So, do we make one last attempt to get out of here, or are we going to Thelma-and-Louise this shit?" ShadowLily slipped her daggers back into their sheaths and held out her hand.

"We ride together, or we die together. Bad girls for life." Cassie thumped her chest. "Just know that I'm totally the Will Smith of our group."

ShadowLily took Cassie's hand in her own. "Well, I do have funny ears."

Looking into her best friend's eyes, she paused when her heels hit the edge. There was nothing behind them but darkness. One more step and they might be dead. The lizard-men moved forward with their shields raised to shove the two women over the edge, but they took the final step themselves.

Chittering laughter filled the air as the women's screams descended into darkness.

CHAPTER THIRTEEN

Where in the hell was everyone?

Tim looked around the inn's main room and saw Ernie and Liz talking to a man at the bar. The rest of the guild was gone. Even JaKobi, who never seemed to leave the inn, was absent from his normal spot at the bar. The Blue Dagger Inn hadn't been this empty in forever. Even on his first day in the game, Gaston had been here with his crew.

Speaking of Gaston's merry men, Tim hadn't seen them in a while. It reminded him that Gaston had a life outside of helping them. He'd have to find out how long the assassin was willing to continue lending them his services. There was always the chance Gaston would want to go back to doing his normal day to day operations now that the inn was safe and Malvonis was off their backs.

Ernie saw Tim standing in the entrance and walked around the bar to come and meet him. "We're waiting on JaKobi to get back before we open up the healing shack." The innkeeper shook Tim's hand. "Until then, Lady Briarthorn sent someone to speak to you about real estate."

"And my two girls? Where did they get off to?" Tim watched

the man at the bar, trying to gain his measure. He was speaking to Liz in a well-mannered way that earned Tim's approval.

"They left in a hurry. Something about Cassie wanting to finish her quest before you came back and ruined her chances for the evening." Ernie sniffed him. "I'd suggest a bath before your meeting, but I know you're in a hurry."

Tim wafted air toward his nose. It wasn't as bad as normal. Leaving the smithy early did wonders for his aroma. "Thanks, Ernie."

The man at the bar stood up as Tim approached and extended his hand in greeting. "Randolph Applebottom, at your service."

"You can call me Tim." He shook the man's hand and motioned for him to join him at a table. "Sorry about my appearance. I just came from my job at the smithy."

Mr. Applebottom waved away his apology. "I understand you are in the market for some real estate?"

"I am." Tim leaned back in his chair. "Lady Briarthorn seems to think you can help me in that regard."

"I should certainly think so. There aren't many people who can do what I do. Working in real estate is more of an art than a science, and I am a very good artist." Randolph tipped his glasses down so he was looking at Tim eye to eye. "Tell me what I can do for you."

Tim tried not to like the man. Mr. Applebottom certainly seemed proud of his real estate prowess, but despite his best efforts, Tim found that he was enjoying his company. "I'd like to find out how much the buildings surrounding the inn are selling for, and what it would cost to repair them."

Randolph smiled. "Acquisition should be easy enough. The crown has been trying to unload most of them for years. As for fixing them up, I'd expect that to take a big slice of your budget." He dropped his excited tone for one more conspiratorial. "How big a budget do we have to work with?"

That was the question, wasn't it. He had a pretty good chunk of gold, but how much was he willing to risk? If his ideas to revitalize the area didn't pan out, he could be losing all the money he'd planned on sending home to his family. If it did work out, he could be set for life.

Was he willing to bet the farm on one roll of the dice?

"Tell me what you think you could accomplish with five hundred gold." It wasn't all his money, but it was enough that if Tim lost it, it would hurt quite a bit.

"I should be able to acquire most of the properties, but it won't be enough for the renovations." Mr. Applebottom looked at Tim with an appraising eye. "How would you like me to proceed?"

"Let's worry about securing the properties for as little as possible, and then we can talk about the cost of renovations. We'll start with the buildings closest to the inn and move outward."

Mr. Applebottom stood and extended his hand. "It seems I have a lot of work to do."

Tim rose and shook the man's hand. "Just keep me up to date, and tell me when I need to make the funds available to you."

"I'll have my banker create an account that we can use for the purchases and to conduct the renovations." He smiled from ear to ear. "Every couple of years, some young entrepreneur comes along and tries to turn this little wasteland into something special. I hope it works out for you."

"Me too." Tim walked him to the door.

Now that he had the place pretty much to himself, he headed for the bathroom and took a quick bath. Despite how much he'd enjoyed bathing since he entered the game, he'd have to talk to one of the contractors about installing a shower. Sometimes taking a bath was just too much work.

Like right now, all he wanted was to take a quick shower to

get the grime off before going to his second job. But instead of a three-minute shower, Tim had to go through an entire process. As he filled the tub, he wondered exactly how much adding a shower would cost.

On the plus side, at least he had access to toilet paper now.

The whole crap-and-piss-in-a-bucket thing left a lot to be desired. That was something they left out of Victorian movies. It wouldn't have been nearly as romantic if you watched people duck into stairwells to take a shit. No wonder there was always someone scrubbing the floors in those manors.

How was it that the Romans had worked out plumbing but the rest of the world used chamber pots?

It was one of the questions you had to ask when you studied history. Maybe people had just gotten to the point they were so busy killing each other that plumbing was the last thing on their lists to worry about.

Every single history book seemed to skip over the famine and struggles of the poor during those days. Now we had a different system. We lifted up our poorest members of society just enough that they see what they were missing out on, while our CEOs raked in the cash.

Not that Tim had anything against making oodles of money.

When it came right down to it, he wanted to make as much money as possible. Not to buy fancy things, but to be in a position where the day to day concerns of how to pay for things went away. Once that happened, he could focus on living life instead of worrying about which bill was more important.

He'd been raised to work hard and to save. He would never buy anything on credit unless it was a car or a house, and both those things together shouldn't be more than fifty percent of his total income. At least business school had taught him how to manage his money. It was a skill that would come in just as handy in the *Etheric Coast* as it did in the real world. Of course, he'd never earn a cent just sitting in the tub.

Tim hopped out of the bath and dried off before equipping his healing outfit. He stepped out of the bathroom and back into the inn's common room. JaKobi was waiting for him, looking a little flushed.

"Sorry I was late." He shrugged in a manner that said it couldn't be helped. "ShadowLily asked me to look into something, and I lost track of time."

JaKobi was kind of a bookworm. If she sent him to do research on something, it was no surprise he'd zoned out. It happened to the best people from time to time when they found something new that captivated their interest.

Tim remembered the first time he'd stayed up all night playing *Final Fantasy*. He'd walked out of the basement as the sun was coming up. His dad was making coffee in the kitchen and gave him a quizzical look before asking, "Were you down there all night?"

The answer, of course, was yes, although Tim didn't confess. Sometimes a little white lie and a long, sleepless day at school were better than losing access to the game. But that was the thing with passion. It didn't matter what you loved, when you loved something and were driven to be the best, you put your heart and soul into it, even if it was just playing a videogame.

When a person got wrapped up in something they loved, time was just a number.

Tim smiled and waved away JaKobi's excuse. "The way I see it, you made it here right on time."

The fire mage looked relieved. "Whatever you say, boss. You ready to head to the shack?"

He wasn't ready, not really. What Tim really wanted was a nap. Working two jobs wasn't for the faint of heart, and if you counted leveling and running his fledgling guild, Tim had three jobs. It was a lot to bear, but if he put in the work for the next couple of years, he'd be able to enjoy the rest of his time in-game.

Three jobs were nothing if it meant retiring in style at forty.

People said to find something you love and you would never work a day in your life, but that wasn't true. Tim loved a lot of things, but anything could feel like a grind. Some days he was sure even Brad Pitt woke up saying, "They want me to play another fucking crazy person?" But when you truly loved something, the passion always came back. There was a certain amount of energy that filled him, and he was ready to take on whatever the day presented.

Tim was ready to embrace the work.

"Let's go." Tim smiled as he stepped into the light drizzle. Things were really starting to come together. If he could get a little lucky, his future was going to be bright. Not just *his* future, but the futures of everyone in the Blue Dagger Society.

Judy had all the people who needed healing lined up. Any injury that needed immediate attention was at the front of the line. After that came anyone he hadn't seen yesterday, then anyone else who showed up.

Tim beamed at the plump older woman's efficiency. "Thanks, Judy. You're doing an amazing job as usual." He pulled out a small purse with thirty silver coins in it. "I believe I owe you a little something extra for the other day."

"It's my pleasure to help." She smiled. "I left a few of those cookies you like on the table in there. Let me know when you're ready, and I'll send the first person in."

"I'm ready now, Judy." Tim made his way into the shack, stuffed a cookie in his mouth, and got ready for his first patient.

The man who came in had a steel rod through his arm. It almost looked like one of the long spikes they hammered into the ground when putting down railroad tracks. Tim hadn't seen or heard any evidence of a train since he'd entered the game, so he wasn't sure what the man had been up to. Sometimes it was more polite not to ask how the injury happened, so he didn't.

That didn't stop his mind from creating stories about what may have happened to the man as he directed him to take a seat on the table so he could get a closer look at the injury. Tim motioned for JaKobi to join him. "Mind holding him down?"

JaKobi came over from his position by the wall and helped the man lie down on the table. The fire mage put his hands on either side of the metal rod and used his weight to push down on the man's arm. "I can tell you from experience that it hurts like hell when he rips it out, but you'll be fine."

"Rips it out—" the patient stammered.

"Trust me." Tim wrapped his fingers around the steel rod and yanked with everything he had. Blood sprayed out of the wound, and the man screamed in pain. Trying to keep his laughter in as the man used a combination of swear words that would make his favorite fictional vampire blush, Tim healed the wound.

The man thanked Tim profusely as he stood up and tested out his arm. He placed a small bag of coins in Tim's outstretched hand. "Thank you."

"It's what I'm here for." Tim smiled warmly at the man and motioned for Judy to escort him outside.

The older woman ran back into of the room, slamming the door shut. Her face was etched with fear. "There are guards coming down the street—a lot of them."

Knowing that he hadn't done anything wrong, Tim wasn't too concerned about the city guards making an appearance, although it did feel a little odd considering how much effort Barry and Chris put into not crossing the archway.

"Why don't we step outside and find out what they want?"

He put a comforting hand on Judy's shoulder. "I'm sure everything is fine."

Judy's pale face didn't inspire him with confidence. He was torn on the subject of law enforcement. In games and fantasy movies, there seemed to be two kinds of guards. There were the evil men and women who worked for a man like the Sheriff of Nottingham, and there were good knights like the ones who worked for King Arthur. There didn't seem to be a lot of ground between the two.

Being a college student with a fondness for beer and parties, Tim had met both kinds of officers. He preferred the laid-back version. Unless there was theft, violence, or murder, Tim's philosophy on law enforcement was the least interaction he had with the law, the better.

Tim liked the number of his total yearly encounters with the cops to rest around zero.

Not having any idea what to expect, but not holding out a lot of hope after meeting Barry and Chris, Tim shot a quick glance at JaKobi and whispered, "Don't do anything stupid."

The fire mage had a pretty level head, but anyone who dabbled in fire magic had a short fuse. Something about working with fire made them temperamental. Tim didn't know what JaKobi's buttons were yet. It was best to not take a chance and give him simple instructions to follow.

Tim stood on the small patio and waited to see where the guards were headed. It didn't take long to see they were coming straight for the shack. There were twenty men, led by what must have been a commander of some type. You could always tell who was in charge by who had on the biggest hat. Or in this case, a hat with a giant feather sticking out of it.

All twenty men had swords on their hips and spears in their hands. They were wearing some kind of hardened leather breastplates, but no other armor. It wasn't the kind of crew you sent to get healing, and none of the men looked injured.

Things were about to get interesting.

"How can I help you today, gentleman?" Tim strode forward, making sure all of the guards' attention was focused on him.

Most of the people waiting for healing suddenly realized they had better places to be as the commander started to speak. "In the name of the crown, I have come to arrest the healer known as Tim."

This had to be fucking Jepsom. The asshole didn't know how to accept no as an answer.

"I'm Tim." He gave JaKobi a quick nod, and the fire mage wrapped an arm around Judy's shoulders and led her off to the side. "Can I ask what I'm being accused of?"

The commander bristled. "Crimes against the temple. The cardinal has provided us with information regarding your illegal healing practice. We are here to take you in."

Tim kept his smile in place, but his mind was racing. With twenty guards, he didn't stand a chance at getting out of this. Plus, he really didn't want to hurt these men. Making an enemy of the crown didn't sound like a very good idea.

"When I spoke with the high priest this morning, I was under the impression that I had his blessing." Tim kept his eyes focused on the commander. "But maybe the cardinal knows more than the man in charge of the goddess' affairs."

The commander paused for a moment. "Please come with us. If what you say is true, I'm sure we'll have this sorted out shortly."

"I hope so. Those people were waiting to be healed, and you've sent them away in pain." Tim turned to JaKobi. "Find the others and tell them what happened."

"We'll come for you as soon as they get back," JaKobi promised, his eyes ringed with orange light.

Tim stepped forward and immediately found himself surrounded by ten men on each side. The commander marched back to the front of the procession and led them into the city. Whatever was happening here wasn't good. If Jepsom was looking to separate him from his friends, he'd done a masterful job.

The cardinal was quickly becoming the one man in the world Tim didn't have any reservations about killing. In fact, the thought of Jepsom's death brought a smile to his face. Tim arched his shoulders back and kept his chin held high. If anyone saw him, he wanted them to know he wasn't afraid.

There was only one person who needed to be worried about their future right now, and these armed guards might be taking Tim directly to him. He had the feeling that when he got to his destination, Jepsom would be there to gloat. Tim, determined not to give him any satisfaction, continued to march as if this was his personal guard and not his prison detail.

Sometimes you just had to roll with the punches.

CHAPTER FOURTEEN

At least Tim wasn't in shackles.

That was the only good thing he could say about his experience. Being escorted from the slums by twenty armed guards seemed like a little much to him. It was the kind of display that was intended to make a point. Jepsom was letting him know just how big a pain in the ass he'd become.

Once he was delivered to the man in charge, Tim would simply explain that the whole situation was a giant misunderstanding. Whoever heard his case had to know that he had the full support of the high priest and that charges from the temple wouldn't stand. Any logical person would have to let him go.

The procession entered a massive courtyard. In its center was a ten-story tower surrounded by smaller buildings on each side. One of the buildings looked like barracks, but the other had guards stationed outside of the door. The tower itself didn't seem big enough to house many prisoners, although it was rather tall, and the solid gray stones made it look very imposing.

As the gate closed behind Tim, the twenty armed guards went back to whatever their duties for the day were. Only the head of his escort remained. He took Tim by the arm and led him to the tower.

Tim didn't see any other prison cells and started to think that maybe the prison was actually below his feet. Being in jail was one thing, being trapped underground in the dark was something else. Starting a new character didn't seem like a bad option when the only other choice was to rot in the dark.

A small shudder of fear made his shoulders tremble. Then he pushed the fear aside and focused on what was right in front of him. If there was any chance of him getting out of this before he saw the inside of a cell, he had to keep his wits about him. Succumbing to the fear of imprisonment now wouldn't do him any favors.

The man who was sent to collect him signaled to a guard by the tower, and the man opened the door for them. Tim went inside first and stopped in the wide circular chamber, unsure of what to do next. The door slammed shut behind him, and the bolt latched in place with a sound of finality that made Tim aware of how badly this could go.

His captor led him to a small desk. The man behind the desk looked to see who had come in and smiled warmly at the officer. "Ah, Captain Reynolds, what brings you to us today?"

Captain Reynolds stood stiffly as if there were a rod jammed up his ass that forced his spine to stay rigidly straight. "I've secured the package for the sheriff. Please inform him that it was done without incident."

"I should hope so. I've never seen a full detachment sent to collect one man. Rather unorthodox, if you ask me," the man at the desk stated flatly.

The captain looked like he was about to answer when a man with a large belly strolled out of a room at the far side of the tower. "That's why nobody asks you anything, Richard."

"Just seems like overkill, Sheriff. I mean, look at him. He's a healer. What was he going to do?" Richard sounded petulant.

"Oh, I'm sure there is much more to him than his profession." The sheriff's eyes roved over Tim. "Or maybe there isn't. It's not my job to question my orders, only to carry them out."

"If there is nothing else, Sheriff, I'd like to return to my post," Captain Reynolds stated in a very matter-of-fact voice.

Tim got the impression the captain wasn't a big fan of the sheriff and wanted to leave as soon as possible.

The sheriff's eyes moved away from Tim and focused on the captain. He extended his hand to the man as a knowing smile lingered at the edges of his mouth. "Thank you for your service, Captain Reynolds. I'll make sure to let your commander know that your performance was satisfactory."

"Thank you, Sir." Captain Reynolds spun on his heel and left the room.

The sheriff turned to Richard. "Send a message to Davros. Our newest acquisition will need to be shown to a cell."

Tim had been watching the proceedings silently, but he couldn't hold his tongue a moment longer. "A cell? Shouldn't there at least be a trial first?"

The sheriff let out a long rumbling belt of laughter. "Did you hear that, Richard? He wants a trial." All the humor faded from his features, and the sheriff's eyes turned hard. "This is where they send people to disappear. There will be no trial. A judgment has already been made, and you will suffer for your sins."

All Tim could think was, *Please don't let me be the next Edmond Dantes.*

Richard frowned. "With all that's going on, Sir, is this the right time to be adding another prisoner?"

"We certainly have the space." The sheriff smiled.

"But with the unexplained deaths, shouldn't we keep him locked in the tower?" Richard almost pleaded.

Unexplained deaths? As if being in prison wasn't bad enough, now he had to worry about something else. The last thing Tim wanted to do was get embroiled in a quest chain at the prison. He didn't have time to figure out this mystery. There was a man of the cloth that needed to meet his demise.

"Oh, I think he'll be fine with the rest of the population." Glaring at Richard, the sheriff slowly nodded his head. "And I don't want to hear anything else about it."

"I'd like to hear more about it," Tim cut in. "If you have men suffering from some kind of illness, maybe I can help."

The sheriff turned his dark, soulless eyes on Tim. "Please join me in my office for a moment." He pointed to the room he previously exited, and from the tone of his voice, Tim knew it wasn't a request.

Tim followed the sheriff into the tiny room and took a seat as he noted the placard resting on the desk, proclaiming it the property of Sheriff Jon Hobbs. Jon's massive belly brushed against Tim as he squeezed around the desk before finally falling into his seat.

This might be Tim's only chance to get a word in, so he decided to go for it. "I think there has been some kind of mistake."

"A mistake? Oh, I don't think so. The cardinal was very clear in his instructions." The sheriff tapped a letter on his table. "He wanted you removed from the equation, and here you are." He opened his hands as if to say, "See, it's simple."

"But I've committed no crime. The healing I've done was sanctioned by the high priest. When he finds out what happened, there will be hell to pay." It was all bluster, but it was the only card Tim had to play.

"Oh, I think not. By the end of today, everyone will have forgotten about you." The sheriff had a sickly sweet smile on his face. "That is what I specialize in—making problems disappear."

Tim scoffed at the notion of him disappearing. "If you wanted to be discreet, you shouldn't have sent twenty men to round me up." Tim noted the little tick above the sheriff's right eye. He'd scored a point. "When my friends find out I'm here, they will come for me."

"We've got plenty of room." Jon Hobbs was back in control now. Being threatened seemed to harden his resolve. "Now, let's get to the business of the day so I can get back to mine, and you can start commiserating about your poor life choices."

The sheriff stood and pointed at a poster on his wall. "The rules are simple. No fighting, no stealing, no bullshit." He tapped the poster. "We count on the prisoners themselves to enforce these rules. The only time you will see any of my men is when it's chow time or when we're dropping in some fresh meat."

Jon had a cruel smile on his face as he pointed at Tim. "You're today's catch."

Tim didn't like the implication that he was fresh meat. Fresh for what, the grinder? He tried to keep his face calm as the sheriff continued his spiel.

"Twice a day, we bring in food, mostly hard biscuits and stew, but every now and then, we splurge, and you get a potato." The sheriff smiled at Tim as if getting a potato should be every man's fondest wish.

I'm totally fucked.

Jon grinned. "I knew you were a potato man." He winked at Tim. "Just between you and me, we might be having them for dinner in honor of your arrival. The other prisoners will be thrilled."

Tim shook his head to clear it. Why was the sheriff giving him the normal "hope you are a model prisoner" shtick when there might be an illness inside of the prison? Didn't he have the right to know?

Raising his hand to interject, Tim spluttered, "So what about these deaths?"

Sheriff Hobbs took a seat. All the good humor he'd been

showing while trying to ruin Tim's life drained from his face. "It's true. We've had something mysterious happening in the dungeon, but I'm not sending any of my men to investigate it."

The sheriff leaned his chair back and rested his hands on his belly. "Frankly, no one's going to miss a few inmates. The only thing I'm worried about is making sure whatever is afflicting them doesn't spread outside these walls."

Something didn't feel right to Tim. This man seemed awfully relaxed, considering there might be some kind of plague brewing under the city. He thought about his trip over here and all of the men he encountered. None of them seemed sick. Was there a chance these men were infecting the prisoners on purpose?

There was no way for Tim to be certain of what was happening. The one thing he did know was that he wouldn't be getting out of this today. For all of his bluster, he was going to be thrown in the dungeon. The last thing he wanted to do before they tossed him in was make the sheriff upset.

"But these are my worries." Jon Hobbs leaned forward, eyes locking onto Tim's like an owl hunting a mouse. "All you have to worry about is following the rules."

"No fighting, no stealing, no bullshit," Tim chanted. "I won't be a problem."

Sheriff Hobbs stood up with a smile on his face that didn't reach his eyes. "See that you aren't. Those boys down there aren't the forgiving sort if you know what I mean."

Tim was pretty sure the sheriff meant that if you got caught stealing down there, it was the last thing you'd ever get caught doing. Watching *Sons of Anarchy* had only taught him that he didn't want to be in prison, not how to deal with it once you were tossed in alone.

"Follow me." The sheriff squeezed past Tim and out into the tower again. He pointed at a man waiting by the door. "This is Davros, and he'll be escorting you to the dungeon. Don't give him any shit, or by God, there won't be another potato served for a month."

Davros stayed just outside of the tower and motioned for Tim to join him. "Right this way."

If he could cast snare on the sheriff and flameburst at Davros, he might be able to make a run for it. Tim's fingers started to twitch through the emotions of snare when he saw the five men training in the yard. There was no way he could take all of them on and win. If he lost, it would only make it harder for his friends to get him out.

Just when things had been going so well, Jepsom had managed to take him off the board before he could do the same to him. Not only was he going to be trapped here, but the clock was ticking. He had seven days to plan and execute the cardinal. Tim wasn't going to be able to do that from inside the dungeon.

"Did the sheriff tell you the rules?" Davros asked as he took Tim's arm to lead him across the courtyard.

"Yeah, no fighting, no—"

Davros cut him off. "Ignore all that shit. Some of these guys are going to test you. If you don't stick up for yourself, you're going to spend the rest of your short life naked and afraid."

He yanked Tim to a stop. "Just don't do it at chow time because the guards will break everyone's skulls, not just yours."

Tim wasn't sure what to say, so he settled for a simple, "Okay."

The dungeon was sounding worse by the minute. First, there was something going on with a disease, and then there was the chance he'd have to win a few fights just to stay alive.

This is why he was getting into real estate and out of being a political assassin.

Tim didn't want to have anything to do with politics and fighting with powerful people. Let the other players have their power. All he wanted to do was make a nice living. It'd be amazing to wake up one day knowing he'd never have to worry about money again.

Not that Tim wanted to live the millionaire lifestyle. He wasn't into flashy things. All he wanted was a nice home to call his own and to make sure his parents could take care of his brother and sister without stressing out. If he could do that, he'd consider himself rich in more ways than one.

Davros opened the gate to a set of stairs leading under the tower. "Sorry about the smell. There isn't a lot of ventilation."

"Might be why the prisoners keep getting sick," Tim quipped before he could stop himself.

"We didn't have any problems before the sheriff went to visit his sister on the other side of the mountains. When he came back, things changed." Davros shrugged, knowing there was nothing he could do about it. "I'd say the sickness is more of a byproduct. The inmates had these marks on their…"

"Ah, Davros, fresh meat for the grinder," a guard inside a second gate called as the two of them approached.

"Sure is, Stan. Make sure he gets in safely. They say he's some kind of healer." Davros motioned for Tim to join the guard inside the gate.

Tim paused before going in. He wanted to know what Davros had been about to tell him, but the man's reaction to the other guard gave him pause. At the last second, he turned his question into gratitude. "Thank—" All the air rushed out of Tim's lungs as Davros' fist slammed into his belly.

"Just remember what I said." Davros shoved Tim toward the entrance.

Lesson number one, don't thank the guards for shit. Tim snickered as his stomach relaxed and it became easier to breathe. Not that the air in here smelled very good. He turned toward the gate, taking one last breath of fresh air before following the guard inside.

The smell inside the dungeon reminded Tim of the time

he'd walked into a room with mold. They weren't kidding when they said that stuff could kill you. Inhaling black mold was toxic in all kinds of ways. He imagined he was being walked into Mold Central. Next thing you know, shit was going to spiral out of control like in *The Andromeda Strain*.

Part of him wanted to believe it was mold or something to do with the dead not being removed from their cells fast enough, but he just couldn't do it. People didn't get funky marks on them from disease. Yes, they could get sores, but marks sounded like something was biting the prisoners.

Stan locked the gate and took a lantern from beside the door. "Let's go."

Tim followed Stan down a set of winding stairs. They reached the bottom four minutes later. Here there was another door, but this time the lock was on their side. Stan put his keys in the lock and opened the passage.

"In you go." Stan made a little shooing motion.

Tim stepped inside the door and jumped as it slammed back into place. This was it, for better or worse; he was inside the dungeon. There was a mysterious illness, and maybe some kind of monster down here.

What could possibly go wrong?

CHAPTER FIFTEEN

"How long has it been?" Cassie asked as she slumped against the wall of the pit.

ShadowLily slid down the dirt wall and sat next to her friend. "Since I sent the message or since we've been down here?"

"Whichever one gets us help first." Cassie used her heels to dig furrows in the ground as she thought about their situation. ShadowLily's class quest had been so easy, it had given her too much confidence in her own. She couldn't stop beating herself up for getting them into this mess. There was no way out of the pit unless the lizard-men let them out.

"It's been three hours since I messaged Tim and JaKobi. I haven't heard anything back." ShadowLily frowned. "And that has me worried. Tim might not be Johnny-on-the-spot with his messages, but he always responds."

Taking a calming breath, the half-elf leaned her head against Cassie's shoulder. "What could they possibly be doing?"

"You've really got it bad, huh?" Cassie asked with a grin. They might be trapped, but it was always the right time to poke fun at your friends.

"What do you mean?" ShadowLily asked as she sat up straight.

Cassie was grinning from ear to ear now. It was dark at the bottom of the pit, so she wasn't sure her bestie could see it, but she was sure ShadowLily would hear it in her voice. "You're so in love with Tim that even while we're stuck in a pit waiting to be eaten by hungry lizard-men, all you're thinking about is if he's okay."

"Oh, shit."

"Oh, shit, indeed." Cassie laughed. "You're in the love zone."

"Better than *The Twilight Zone?*" ShadowLily snarked before gently leaning the back of her head against the wall of the pit. "When did this happen?" Then, in a more panicked tone, "Do you think he feels the same way?"

"Girl, you've had him locked up since day one. Only way you're getting rid of him now is if you burn him off like a leech." The tank hopped to her feet and started pacing the pit. She hated being still, and that was why she couldn't wait for them to become adventurers. No more of this going-to-work shit. They were going to be epic.

ShadowLily would have smacked Cassie if she could see her. "Gross."

"It's true. He's stuck on you like gum on the bottom of your shoes." Cassie smiled again. "And we all know how hard that shit is to get off."

ShadowLily was starting to come out of her shock. "There should be a law against people spitting their gum on the sidewalk."

"The first execution in what has been dubbed by some on social media as the bubble gum disposal act will air live tonight at nine." Cassie started to giggle. "Problem solved. No one is going to risk spitting that shit on the sidewalk ever again."

"At least *The Etheric Coast* is safe from those horrible criminals. They don't have gum or sidewalks here." ShadowLily extended her hands out and brought them together like she was a giant crocodile. "Imagine how those lizards would look with a mouthful of gum."

"That shit would go viral on Twitter for sure. People would look at one another at work and be like, hey, did you see that video where the lizard was trying to chew gum?" Cassie brushed off the seat of her pants. She had a thing about being dirty; she didn't like it one fucking bit.

Gazing up into the darkness, Cassie shouted, "Hey, lizard-for-brains." She took a deep breath and then belted, "Any chance we can hurry this the fuck up?"

No one responded to her shout, and Cassie slammed her fist into the hard-packed earth of the wall. "I wish they'd just get it over with. This waiting around shit is killing me."

ShadowLily patted the ground next to her. "Why don't you try to get some rest? When they come for us, we're going to need our energy."

Cassie sat down and cuddled against her friend. Her mind was spinning, and she was worried they might not actually make it out of this. Despite the parade of random thoughts circling her mind, the little tank's eyes started to close. All that running must have really taken it out of her.

Orange light flickered through the darkness, stinging Cassie's eyes.

"Why in the fuck is it so bright?" Cassie looked at Shadow-Lily, and a chorus of drums sounded from overhead.

The drums had the effect of putting her on edge, but not as much as the giant cage the lizard-men had lowered into the pit while they'd been sleeping. The cage was made out of bent branches tied together with thick green vines. Stuck out in a circle around the cage were five torches.

After sleeping in the dark for so long, the lights seemed impossibly bright. "You think the green bastards would have a little more respect for the two finest ladies they've ever laid eyes on," Cassie groused as she blinked.

ShadowLily walked over to the cage to inspect it. "I think we're supposed to get in.

"No way." Cassie scrambled to her feet. "There isn't a horror movie out today where climbing into a cage had a happy ending. Shit, even in the Disney movies, getting in a cage normally means someone is trying to eat you."

ShadowLily looked at the lip of the pit fifteen feet above their heads. "It's not like we have a choice. Unless you've thought of another way to get out of here?"

"It's not like anyone could think with all that racket." Cassie motioned above them, indicating the relentless sound of the drums. She joined ShadowLily by the door. "Let's just do it."

"I'm happy you said that. That way, when this all turns to shit, I can blame you. I always find it feels better not to be the one who fucked up." ShadowLily opened the door to the cage and stepped inside. "I can't believe the boys back at the inn never messaged us back. There is going to be retribution, but not until I get an ice-cold beer."

"Shit," Cassie blurted as she joined ShadowLily in the wooden cage. "I haven't checked my messages since we got up." It took her a few seconds to get her user interface open and another brief moment before her messages displayed in front of her. There was one new message from JaKobi.

We're on the way.

The timestamp on the message indicated it was from four hours ago. Either they'd never made it here, or they were waiting in a pit just like them. Maybe they should not have asked for help. Adding more deaths to her conscience wasn't going to make her feel any better. Against so many lizard-men, their entire guild working together might not have survived the first wave of battle.

"JaKobi sent me a note that said they were coming." She closed the cage door. "I don't think they made it."

"And you didn't get anything from Tim?" ShadowLily asked worriedly.

"Nope, but I'm sure he's fine. Probably too busy working on one of his harebrained schemes to check his messages." Cassie looked around and wondered when their ride to the surface would begin.

"I hope you're right." ShadowLily looked morose as the cage jerked violently. Once they were moving, the cage settled, making it easy for them to stand without falling over. Getting to the top after falling on their asses wouldn't give the right impression.

The cage continued to rise smoothly as if they were being pulled up by a winch of some sort. The drums continued to get louder as they drew closer to the surface. Finally, they were lifted above the pit. Both women gasped as they looked at the scene below them.

They were in a wide-open clearing. The jungle's thick grass had been chopped or flattened. There was a throne inside the bottom half of a giant lizard's jaw. The teeth rose over the chair like an arch with spikes. Sitting on the throne was an enormous lizard-man. The chieftain's arms and legs were painted vibrant colors, and he wore a headdress made out of colorful feathers.

The chieftain only kept Cassie's attention for a moment. She could deal with one giant bastard, but what she couldn't deal with were the hundreds of lizard-men gathered in the clearing.

Was this some kind of celebration? If it was a celebration of some sort, the question quickly became, were they the guests of honor or dinner?

The cage was lowered to the ground, and the door opened by one of the lizard soldiers. He pointed toward the throne. When the two of them didn't start walking, he nudged them forward with the tip of his spear.

"We get it already." Cassie slammed her open palm down on his spear. "If you touch me with that thing, I'm going to kick your fucking ass."

The lizard-man's tongue flicked out around his teeth, and there was a sound coming from his throat that might have been laughter. He pointed over their heads again and lifted his shield to give them another push in the right direction.

Cassie glared at their captor. "Try it."

ShadowLily put a calming hand on Cassie's shoulder. "We've got bigger things to be concerned about."

"But kicking his ass would make me feel so much better." Cassie turned to see what could possibly be worse than being surrounded by hungry-looking lizard-men.

It didn't take her long to see what ShadowLily was worried about. Standing at the base of the throne were Gaston and JaKobi. Both men had their hands tied in front of them. It didn't escape her attention that each of them had been assigned their own guard, while the sexist lizards only assigned a single escort for the two of them.

"Chauvinist fucks," Cassie grumbled. "Just let me go *mano a mano* with one of these green bastards, and they'll learn not to underestimate a woman."

"Maybe we can worry about satisfying your ego after we're safe." She kept her eyes locked on the throne. "Tim's not here. Where in the hell is he?"

"Working on a secret plan?" Cassie sure hoped that was what Tim was doing. Right about now, they could use one of his great ideas to get the hell out of here.

They stopped at the base of the throne as the chieftain watched them. "Coming into the hidden forest is a death sentence. The four of you will be sacrificed to appease Havithor, the Great Worm. With your lives comes peace and prosperity for our people."

Cassie spat on the ground. "I desire a trial by combat." It was worth a try. That shit always worked in the movies.

The weird laughter chittered from all around them. The chieftain walked down the steps toward Cassie. Stopping in front of her, he smiled. "I will grant one of you the right to face our champion. Win, and all of you shall be spared. Lose, and all of you will become willing sacrifices to the Great Worm."

Cassie stood as tall as she could. Her eyes shot daggers at the chieftain. There wasn't an inch of back-down in her. "Bring it on, Puff. I need a new pair of boots."

The chieftain chuffed his laughter. "Wouldn't you prefer one of your champions to take your place?" He pointed at the two men with their wrists bound in front of them.

Gaston nudged JaKobi's shoulder. "He doesn't know how bad he just fucked up."

"Right. One time I asked Ernie for a small serving, and she thought I was making a joke about her. My arm hurt for a week. That lizard just implied a woman wouldn't stand a chance against their champion. Cassie's going to wipe the floor with him."

The chieftain followed the two men's conversation before turning his confused gaze on Cassie. "So it will be you who faces Drago?"

"Drago's about to be my bitch!" Cassie scanned the crowd. "Which one of you is it?" she shouted in defiance.

The chieftain walked back up the steps to his throne. He lifted his arms and the drumming stopped. "The sacrifices have asked for the right to fight our champion, and I have granted them the opportunity." He snickered before looking across the clearing. "I call on Drago the Destroyer to represent the clan."

A cheer rose from the crowd and they scrambled to line the

clearing, leaving one path to a hut set at the far edge. The drums started to play again, but this time their rhythm was different. This time the drums summoned their champion to war.

Cassie heard them shouting the name "Drago" over and over. She wasn't sure what all the hype was about. Looking around the crowd didn't show her a lot of difference between one lizard-man and another. Unless Drago was some kind of freak, she'd be fine.

A large gray shape came out of the hut. At first, she thought it was a massive sculpture, something to show them just how badass their champion was, but then she realized it was him. The giant lizard-man had to walk out of the hut sideways. As he turned to face them, he rolled his massive shoulders.

Drago was easily twice as wide as the rest of the lizard-men, and Cassie wouldn't have been surprised to find out he was at least nine feet tall. The massive beast shrieked into the sky, and the drums started to play faster. The lizard-men near the hut formed a circle.

The chieftain looked at Cassie with a smug smile etched on his features. "Our champion awaits."

Cassie pulled her bō staff from her inventory and twirled it. She cast a withering look at the chieftain and did her best Samuel L. Jackson impression. "I've had it with these motherfucking lizards in this motherfucking game."

With one last look at her friends, Cassie stalked forward to meet Drago in the circle of champions.

CHAPTER SIXTEEN

Thankfully, there were torches in the dungeon.

Tim forced a nervous smile on his face. Sometimes in life, it paid to be grateful for what you had and not be concerned with what you wanted. Being trapped down here without a single torch would have been infinitely more miserable than it was right now.

After what Davros said, Tim had been expecting to be ambushed by the other prisoners the very second he entered the dungeon, but he hadn't seen one of them yet. He wasn't sure exactly what he envisioned, but it had been more like the scene in *The Chronicles of Riddick* than the silent welcome he was receiving now.

He moved deeper into the dungeon without revealing anything new. The walls were made out of roughhewn stone blocks, and the stones didn't always match. Either some of them had been replaced over the years, or they used stone from multiple quarries to make the dungeon. Despite the general smell of dampness, the stone walls and ceiling appeared to be dry.

A long, raspy moan echoed down the hall from somewhere in the darkness.

It was the kind of sound you'd hear in a ghost movie right before something came out of the walls and chased you down. Tim realized that there could be ghosts in the game. Almost every type of fantasy game had some version of the undead in it. Who else were the clerics going to smite with their holy light?

That being said, he generally wasn't scared of dark and creepy places. He was more of a "have to see it to believe it" kind of guy. At least, that was what he liked to tell himself, but if you put him in a cemetery late at night, added a little fog to the ground, and something brushed against him, he'd run away faster than everyone else.

You gotta be realistic about these things.

Tim pulled his staff out of his inventory and readied his *flameburst* spell. If he rounded a corner and a bunch of people tried to rob him, there were going to be a few crispy motherfuckers down here.

Hell, yeah, he was ready to rumble, baby!

Instead of a corner at the end of the hall, there was a dark wooden door. Tim grabbed the thick iron ring and pulled the door open. Another moan filled the air. This time it sounded more like a man getting a limb cut off in a civil war movie than a ghost. He forgot all about being worried and rushed into the room to help in any way he could.

Four men were huddled around a bundle of straw on the floor. A fifth man was lying there, and that was who was making the god-awful sound. The other men seemed to be trying to hold him down as he writhed in pain. One of them had a rag and a bucket of water and was washing the sweat from the sick man's forehead.

"What's going on here?" Tim asked.

Two of the four men jumped away from the man on the

floor, making the sign of the goddess over their chest. The other two looked at Tim with their jaws hanging open in shock. From the looks on all of their faces, they didn't expect to get out of the room alive.

Now that he'd given all of them a heart attack, Tim tried to sound friendly as he spoke. He pointed at himself. "New arrival. Sorry if I startled you."

"That bastard Hobbs is still bringing people down here? Jordan, I told you we needed to try to kill that fucker the last time he was down here."

"Simmer down, Henry. That was five years ago. It's not like killing Hobbs would do anything but make it harder on all of us. You know damn well they'd just find an even bigger asshole to takeover."

Jordan turned to look at Tim. "If you haven't heard yet, there's something going on down here, and I'd say dollars to doughnuts the sheriff is behind it."

Henry motioned for the other men to take his place by the man on the floor. "The sheriff has never been anything to us but uninterested. As long as we don't kill each other, he's never given a shit about us."

Tim took a step forward. "Do you mind if I take a look at him? I'm a healer by trade. There might be something I can do."

"I told you the goddess would provide," Henry said, making Her sign over his chest before motioning Tim forward.

Leaning down, Tim started to examine the man's arms and legs. "One of the guards mentioned some of the afflicted had marks on them. Have you seen anything like that?"

"There's something on the back of his neck. We've never seen anything like it before," Henry chimed in as he bent down to help roll the injured man over.

The moan that escaped from the man's mouth broke Tim's heart. He'd always been fine with being in pain himself, but he hated seeing others in pain. There was something about seeing someone hurt that made him want to help them. He probably should have tried to be a doctor back in the real world, but who had time for all the extra classes when there was beer to be drunk?

The marks on the back of the man's neck weren't like anything Tim had seen before either. All he could say for certain was that he was fairly sure they weren't dealing with a vampire. There were three marks at the base of the man's neck. He took the wet rag and wiped the crusted blood away, but still couldn't make sense of them.

Tim looked at the men gathered around. "I'm not sure what happened to him, but I might be able to help." He motioned for the men to step back and started casting cleanse.

On the fourth cast of the spell, a foul-smelling white pus leaked from the wound on his patient's neck. The man on the ground let out a strangled cry, then his body went still. Tim watched him for a few moments, afraid that he might have killed him. He splashed a healing orb against him and hoped for the best.

The four men in the room were staring at him. One of them had a look on his face that said, "If he's dead, so are you." Doing his best to ignore them, Tim kept his eyes locked on the man he'd healed. His chest had started to move, but he wasn't awake yet.

At least I didn't kill him.

When his eyes fluttered open, the men in the room jumped back from the body like they'd seen a ghost. Or maybe they were worried about zombies. Oh, shit, did this game have zombies?

Tim held out his hand. "Water. I need water."

Henry ran out of the room and came back a moment later with a skin that had the stopper removed. Tim took it from him and leaned over the man on the ground to help him drink. Maybe the goddess really did have a hand in all things. It was starting to feel like he'd been sent here to help these men. It wasn't like the saints from the real world got there by tending to the affluent.

They were considered saints because they'd helped everyone.

Not that he thought of himself as a saint, or even saintly. It took a certain kind of selflessness to reach that level of divinity, something he didn't have. Yes, he had a strong desire to help people, especially those less fortunate, but Tim also liked his things and his alone time.

That part of him he would have to give up to become saintly wasn't something he was ready to part with just yet. Plus, his life was already pretty awesome. He was in a new reality with the woman he loved. Here he could heal people and lead a group. Back home, he would have been the lowest man on the financial totem pole in a giant corporation.

One of the forgotten.

Tim extended his hand to the man he'd healed and pulled him into a sitting position. "How are you feeling?"

"Better now that I'm awake." He looked at the five men huddled around him. "Thanks for not leaving me to die."

Jordan leaned down next to him. "None of us knew what to do, Tony." He stopped talking and pointed at Tim. "Hobbs arrested this healer, and he saved you."

"Fucking Hobbs," Tony mumbled. "Hate having to be grateful to that bastard for anything."

"Then don't be." Tim smiled at the man. "I hate that fucker too."

"From the goddess' lips to my ears," Tony said with a smile. He looked around the room, and his smile quickly faded. "Do we have anything to eat?"

Henry slapped him on the back. "Of course, this crazy fucker wakes up, and the first thing he asks about is food."

Jordan helped Tony to his feet. "I'm sure we can wrangle

something up. If not, it's almost chow time." He pointed at Tim. "The new arrival means potatoes tonight."

Tony shuddered. "I swear to the gods it's a good thing we found another use for those potatoes, or I would have gone nuts by now. But the goddess has her ways." He elbowed the man next to him. "Doesn't she, boys?"

Tim laughed out loud at the men's antics, wondering what exactly they did with their potatoes. He actually loved potatoes. There were so many ways you could make them: baked, twice baked, smashed, mashed, or fried. They always tasted awesome, and they were one of the cheapest fillers you could buy, although a steady diet of spuds did sound horrible. There had to be something he was missing.

Did Sheriff Hobbs think he was Penn?

That crazy comedian had eaten nothing but potatoes for three months. Sometimes you gotta do what you gotta do to lose weight, but restricting your diet like that would break Tim in a week, if he made it that long. He needed real food, even if it meant having to exercise.

Henry wrapped an arm around Tim's shoulders. "Plus, we have to introduce fresh meat here to the rest of the boys."

Looking at each of the men in turn, Tim felt like they might just be screwing with him. At least his first day in the dungeon wasn't going to be filled with running away from hordes of hungry sex-starved men in fear. He might even be able to spend his time here doing something useful. "Is there anyone else who needs healing?"

Jordan smiled. "Oh, I'm sure some of the guys will take you up on that offer. We don't usually get visits from the healers down here." His gaze narrowed on Tim like a grandma spotting her favorite yarn on sale at the hobby store. "Maybe with you here, we can finally get to the bottom of what's going on."

"Any chance you're up for helping us?" Jordan extended his hand toward Tim.

Quest Received: Something Wicked this Way Comes

There is something strange happening in the dungeon. The guards and the sheriff are calling it a mysterious illness, and yet there are rumors that the illness is caused by some kind of attack. Your job is to find out the truth and put an end to whatever is going on.

Accept Quest: Yes/No

Tim accepted the quest. If he was going to be trapped here for a few days, he might as well get some experience out of it. There was always a chance his friends would find a way to get him out of here earlier, so he could always abandon the quest chain or come back and do the quest later.

There was also a part of Tim that didn't want to be too involved. He didn't want anyone to die, but he certainly didn't want to make life more comfortable for criminals. Although, with how he'd been spirited away, it was more than likely at least a few of these men were down here for doing the right thing.

Not all of them could be innocent, though, not with the prison right in the city. Somebody would have surely noticed the dungeon filling up without any criminals being tried. If working through the monarchy was anything like working through the government, maybe no one took the time to notice. The sheriff could have a nice profitable side business going right under the kingdom's nose.

Innocent or not, something was attacking these men. Tim believed, at the very least, every prisoner needed to be safe from physical threats. Being eaten or fed on seemed to meet his threshold for demanding justice. No one was going to be eaten while he was here.

Criminals or not, he wouldn't stand for a monster feeding on these men.

The five inmates led him down a long hallway. There were branches going in multiple directions, but they continued in a straight line. At the end of the hallway was another wooden door, although this one was open and you could hear boisterous shouting and singing coming from beyond.

Tim stepped into a large common room. With all of the raised mugs, he might as well have stepped back into the Blue Dagger. Sacks of potatoes lined one wall, and against another, there was some kind of contraption that must have been a still. They were making alcohol out of the potatoes.

No wonder these guys got fucking excited about potato night.

Given how the rest of the prisoners were acting, he would not have thought there was a sickness down here. Tim took a few steps into the room and craned his neck to see what everyone was looking at. On the floor in the center of the room was a black cloth with a man lying on it. He started listening to the songs being sung and realized this wasn't a party, but a funeral.

"If you'd been arrested yesterday, Khris might still be with us," Henry said as he handed Tim a drink. "As you can tell, everyone contributes their potato rations to the still. The fuckers upstairs think we love to eat the damn things, but we use them to make vodka."

Tim took a sip of his drink and coughed so hard tears leaked from his eyes. He looked into Henry's smiling face. "Strong stuff."

"The stronger, the better I say." Henry clinked his glass against Tim's and wandered off to join the proceedings.

The shot of potato vodka in Tim's belly was warming him up nicely. He kept his eyes moving around the room. It was kind of like being invited to a massive house party when you only knew one person. Clinging to the person you came with like a flotation device was frowned upon. At some point, you had to branch out and mingle or go home.

Going home wasn't an option, so Tim had to talk to a few people. He'd had problems breaking the ice with other college students, but now he was about to do it with thieves, rapists, and murderers.

Tim chuckled for a moment. Technically, he was a murderer and a thief, so as long as none of the guys down here were rapists, he might be in okay company. It was funny how that line differed in the game. Killing for the right reasons in the game could make you a hero, but back in the real world, it only made you a serial killer.

Even *Dexter* lived with the fear of getting caught.

But Tim's favorite serial killer only went after the bad guys. Dexter always reserved a little extra time to make sure his victims knew he was there for a reckoning, just like Tim believed there was a special place in hell for rapists and the people who hurt children. Hopefully, one where men like Dexter killed them a hundred times a day.

Tim looked around the room's tall stone walls and dirty floors and muttered, "This dungeon is too good for those worthless fuckers."

There were some crimes that Tim considered so horrific you shouldn't be let out. In his mind, rape was the worst crime, and seeing people get off with such light sentences had always rubbed him the wrong way. The person who was raped didn't get a redo after a few years in a box. They had to deal with their wounds for the rest of their lives.

It just didn't seem fair. Lock those fuckers up in a jail that only housed other rapists and call it a day.

Tim was startled out of his thoughts when Tony touched his arm. He almost jumped but managed to stop himself at the last moment. "What's up?" He tried to smile, covering his freak out so smoothly they should have called him "Iceman."

Tony watched him for a moment and then flicked his eyes to the man standing next to him. "This is Baron. He's in charge of our merry band."

"Merry might be too nice a word for it," Baron said in a

baritone voice that could have competed with James Earl Jones for top honors. "We're mostly just trying to survive."

"Ah, it's not that bad." Tony pointed at Tim. "Tell him how you saved my ass."

Taking another sip from his drink, Tim coughed again. Between gasps, he managed to choke out the word, "Healer." Ok, so maybe his smoothness wasn't at peak levels today.

Baron grinned. "It's vile stuff, but it's the best we can do." He motioned for Tim to join him in the corner where there was a little less ruckus. "So tell me honestly, have you ever seen anything like this?"

"No, and I've seen a lot of stuff." Tim didn't think the wound was from a weapon. The only logical explanation was something supernatural, but he couldn't think of anything offhand that left those kinds of marks on someone's neck.

Back home, he'd been a horror movie nerd. He had a personal rating system for scary movies. There was a "fuck no" pile for movies that were so bad you wondered why someone had invested in them. That pile of movies never got watched again and normally ended up in the trash.

No way he was donating them to perpetuate the cycle of shittiness.

The next pile was the "I watch those while doing other stuff" grouping. This included movies that had barely escaped the "fuck no" pile, but also a few that hadn't earned the right to be in the "watch with reverence" stack.

So when Tim said he'd seen a lot of stuff, he meant it. He'd seen every harebrained idea out there, and all the classics, not to mention however many billion seasons of the Winchesters hunting down just about everything. Even with all his knowledge of the macabre, he still couldn't figure this out.

There were plenty of things out there that liked to snack on humans, though. The undead wouldn't have left anything behind, vampires normally hit the major arteries, and werewolves just kind of fucked people up, they didn't necessarily eat them. There was always the chance it was paranormal since all kinds of things feed on people's essence.

There was no way to know what they were dealing with unless they could catch the thing in the act of feeding. At that point, they'd either know what it was and be able to stop it, or they'd be next up on the menu.

"Anything you can do to help us stop another one of these attacks from happening would be greatly appreciated." Baron looked at the men in the room. "These might not be the best men in Promethia, but they are my friends."

"Do you know if any of the other victims had marks on their necks? I wonder if they have to be attacked a few times to end up like Tony or if it only has to happen once." Tim turned away from the crowd to focus on Baron's response.

"We haven't checked anyone who hasn't gotten sick. The first sign seems to be moaning in their sleep. After a few nights of that, they get a fever, and then they die. The guards come and collect the bodies." Baron looked lost in thought.

"How many men have died?" Tim took another sip of his drink, preparing himself for the answer.

Baron took a long swallow from his own cup. "At least fifteen, maybe more. Sometimes people like to be alone down here. We can't keep track of everyone."

"When there is the time we should round everyone up so we can check their necks." Tim ran a hand through his hair, brushing it behind his ears. "Then maybe we can find something that links them together. Anything could be important. Where they sleep. Are they alone? Maybe even what they eat and drink."

"If we can figure out how these men are being targeted, we might have a chance of stopping this thing." Baron looked at the men mourning the loss of a friend. He took a sip from his drink, and a sad smile spread across his face. "Let's let the men have the night. We'll get started first thing in the morning."

Tim found a quiet corner with a little bit of straw he formed into a bed. He covered it in his cloak and sat down. He continued nursing his drink as he thought about what he had to do here. Then he realized he also had to be ready to take care of the Jepsom issue if his friends busted him out.

He pulled out the information Paul had given him and started looking it over. His mind kept wandering to the more immediate problem of staying alive long enough to escape, so he set the file aside and rested his head against the wall. It was always easier for him to think with his eyes closed.

He'd find a way to get through this. Tim wasn't ready for his story to be over just yet.

CHAPTER SEVENTEEN

Big motherfuckers make more noise when they fall.

Cassie grinned as the thought circled through her mind. The quest she was on wouldn't have led her to this cave if there wasn't a way for her to win, and the way out was walking toward the center of the clearing now. When she beat the overstuffed lizard, they would be out of here and back to the inn before you could order a pizza.

Why is thirty minutes or less still not a thing?

Circle of Champions was an apt description, but cage match would have been closer to the truth. There was a thirty foot dome of vines being slowly lowered over the area they were going to fight in. The dome might be in place just to make sure the contestants couldn't run, but Cassie had the feeling the vines might be strategic as well.

Not that Drago needed an extra strategy to beat her. Big lizard smashes small girl might be the headline on the news at eleven, but not if she could help it. A much more rewarding story would be her kicking Drago's gray-skinned ass back into the egg he was hatched from.

ShadowLily, Gaston, and JaKobi had their hands bound in

front of them and were standing off to the side to watch the battle. Guess the lizard king wanted to make sure they didn't try to run if she lost. No one would walk willingly into a worm's maw, but that was their only option if she didn't come through.

They didn't make sunscreen strong enough to ward off lava.

Everything was riding on Cassie, but she was used to that. As a tank in games, most of the responsibility was always on her shoulders. She had to be able to make calls and avoid all the crap on the ground while making sure none of the DPS pulled the boss off her. It was a lot of work, and not everyone was cut out for it.

But Cassie was.

She could lead a group and was willing to take a hit for the team when necessary. Right now her team was counting on her to go toe to toe with Drago and come out on top. No way would she fucking let them down. Cassie had ice in her veins and lady-balls big enough to choke a hippopotamus.

The door to the dome was right in front of Cassie now. She gave a curt nod to her friends and walked inside. The grass in this area was trimmed like they had brought in the ground crew from Augusta National. The ground looked perfectly flat and perfect for combat. She scanned the manicured grass, but nothing looked out of place. If the lizard-men had rigged the arena somehow, the surprise wouldn't be coming from below her.

The only thing she couldn't be certain of was how or if Drago would use the vine-y canopy above them.

There was no way Cassie would be able to use the vines to her advantage. By the time she scrambled high enough to do anything, Drago would be all over her. Those sharp claws on his hands and feet made him a much better climber, and his size made him faster than her.

Size wasn't everything, though.

Cassie could turn on a dime and duck under a lot of things with ease. Drago would never be able to slow down his bulk fast enough to catch her. Plus, she was getting better at dealing with her inferior reach. It was part of why she had chosen to go with the bō staff instead of a more traditional sword-and-board play style.

With a sword and a shield, she might never get the chance to hit an opponent, which was kind of important for a tank. The last thing she wanted was to be rooted in place. She'd learned a long time ago that there was always someone bigger and stronger than you. Shit, some of those guys on late-night TV pulled buses.

Cassie wasn't built for that, and wearing all that bulky armor would just slow her down. So instead of carrying all that crap, she wore leather and had her custom-made shin and forearm guards. She could block with all her limbs but was still light enough to move quickly.

Her speed and size were what gave her the chance to win.

When Drago entered the arena, the lizard-men around the perimeter started chanting his name. The beast raised his hands above his head and let out a fierce roar that would have made Godzilla jealous. He slapped his chest with one fist, and the men outside did the same.

Cassie watched the door to the arena be sealed shut and tied closed with fresh vines. There was no way she was getting out of this alive unless she won. The odds looked like they were stacked against her, but she'd never been a big believer in odds.

Sometimes you had to make your own luck.

She pointed at her three guildmates as they huddled together to watch her through a gap in the vines. Cassie made eye contact with ShadowLily and nodded in a way that said, "Don't worry about a thang. I've got you."

The lizard king climbed to the top of the dome and held his hands up to silence the crowd. "Drago has been challenged. To the winner goes freedom!" The crowd cheered wildly. "The loser will be sacrificed to appease the Great Worm!"

Soaking up the adulation of his people, the king lifted one hand and pointed toward Drago. "Are you ready?"

Drago roared, and some of the men outside of the dome cringed in fear.

The king turned his attention to Cassie. "Ready to meet your goddess?"

Cassie smirked at the king perched high overhead. "I've already had the pleasure." She shrugged. "Seemed as though she wasn't ready for me to die."

"The rules are simple. Two champions enter, one leaves." Green light started to pool around the king's hands. He brought them in front of his chest, then held them out as if he were cradling something before he broke apart his palms like he was letting water fall back into the basin.

A single neon-green leaf fluttered slowly toward the ground.

"The match will begin when the leaf hits the floor." The king lifted his staff and let out a cry. The drums went silent. The night was so still that it felt like everyone was holding their breath. Every single eye watched the leaf ride the gentle breeze as it fell toward the grass.

The leaf continued its inevitable descent, and Cassie got ready. This was it, ready or not. Drago was coming for her. Cassie made sure her armor was tied tightly in place before digging her back foot into the soft earth. She was ready to move the second the leaf hit the ground.

This big fucker wasn't going to know what hit him.

Drago laughed when the leaf hit the ground. With total disregard for Cassie, he extended his arms toward the barrier. A shield and a spear were lowered through the vines. The giant lizard turned with weapons in hand and snapped his jaws. The crowd grew silent as their champion focused on the tiny human.

It took all of Cassie's self-control not to fall for the bait. Who knew that lizard-for-brains would be smart enough to try to lay a trap? Fighters who rushed into Drago's taunts probably lost quickly. For her, this was a battle of endurance. The best person would be the last one standing.

Not that she didn't want to rush over there and clunk the fucker on the head.

But she was a tank. Her will was made of granite. She would stand like a pillar of earth in the face of certain death. Cassie would not give in to her desire to attack. She would wait for the bastard to come to her, then show him what it meant to be her bitch.

Drago walked forward, and the crowd erupted. Their champion pandered to them for a moment before raising his shield and narrowing his focus on Cassie. He turned slightly so his bulk was behind the giant slab of wood and shuffled toward his target with practiced steps.

The bastard was getting closer, but Cassie wasn't going to let him have all the fun. She twirled her bō staff around her in wicked-looking spirals before tucking it against her back. She extended one palm toward Drago and gave him the classic "bring it on" gesture.

Lizard-for-brains wasn't the only one who could play games.

Three human voices cheered Cassie from behind. She smiled and knew that no matter what, her friends had her back. All she had to do now was be confident in her abilities and trust that this had been set up to test her skills, not make her regret every choice she'd made since coming into the game.

As an avoidance tank, standing in one place might as well have been a death sentence, so Cassie started to circle. Drago matched her, circling with ease and kept his shield aimed at her midsection and his spear raised in his other hand, ready to strike.

This was going to be a long fight if neither of them tried to engage, but the longer the fight lasted, the better it would be for Cassie. That shield looked heavy, and so did all those muscles. There was a difference between being in shape and being incredibly bulky. Bulky muscles were created for short bouts of epic strength, whereas a yoga-like physique had stamina for days.

Cassie reached into her belt and threw a dagger at Drago. The blade slammed into his wooden shield and stuck there like an exclamation point. The giant lizard-man smiled over the rim of his shield as though he'd won some great victory.

Let him think that. Cassie smiled. Her mind was starting to work like Tim's. Her plan was to appear to be less than she was and get Drago to chase her around. Finally, when he was tired, she'd fuck him up. The name of the game was endurance, and she had loads of it.

Drago rushed forward, closing the distance between them in two steps. His shield went out to bash her, but Cassie rolled out of the way. She came up on his side ready, to give him a thumping, only to find the point of spear coming right at her. Her staff deflected the spear thrust and she was moving again.

Despite being so big, the lizard-man was quick. She hadn't thought he'd be able to turn as fast as he had. Maybe he used his tail for balance, which let him recover faster than a human could. Going forward, Cassie would have to keep that in mind. There weren't going to be a lot of opportunities to deliver punishment until Drago got tired.

Keeping that in mind, Cassie started to circle him again, and with each step, she angled herself farther away. She grinned at the lizard, almost laughing at her blade quivering in his shield. If the fucker knew how long it had taken her to learn how to throw that knife, he would have been impressed.

Roaring with fury, Drago charged. His spear slashed forward again and again. Cassie skipped and rolled, using her bō staff to shift the tip of the spear out of the way. There were a few close calls, but so far, she'd been able to keep him off balance, and now his movements seemed to be taking longer.

Cassie scored her first hit when Drago overextended his spear arm. Her staff connected with his wrist, there was a crack like the sound of ice breaking on a frozen lake, and Drago's spear fell to the ground.

Drago roared in pain as he took his shield in both hands and used it like a bat.

Cassie hadn't expected to be assaulted by a wall of wood, not when she was pretty sure the big fucker was down to one healthy wrist. There was nothing she could do to get out of the way. The only thing she had left was to try to roll with the hit.

The shield cracked her in the side, and Cassie flew across the arena. The grass cushioned her fall as she turned it into a roll. She climbed back to her feet after learning what it felt like to get hit by a bus. Drago was smiling at her, and all she wanted to do was rip the smug grin off his face.

People had been smiling at her like that her whole life. When she walked into a room, because she was pretty and tiny, people forgot about her. Well, this shit-licking dragon fucker wasn't going to get the best of her.

The crowd cheered as their champion tossed his shield away. He bent down, picked up his spear with his left hand, and started jogging toward Cassie. She kept her eyes focused on him. It had been easy to keep him away when Drago had the shield, but without it, he could just wrap his arms around her.

Getting smothered to death seemed like a shitty way to go.

It was hard not to sprint forward and meet his charge. She kept circling and adding distance between them. He wasn't nearly as proficient with the spear in his left hand as he had been with his right.

Thankfully for Cassie, that meant she'd done some damage with her lone strike of the fight. If Drago couldn't hold the spear in his right hand, it gave her something to work with.

The king screamed at Drago as his next attack missed Cassie completely. A blue orb fell from the top of the dome, fluttering toward the injured lizard-man. Cassie rushed forward, pulling her hook and chain from her belt. She took aim when the blue orb was fifteen feet away from Drago's outstretched hand.

The hook spiraled through the air, wrapping around Drago's ankle before latching onto the chain. Cassie yanked for everything she was worth and watched Drago stumble to his knees. Dropping the chain to the floor, she sprinted toward the fallen fighter with every ounce of strength she could summon. With a cry, she leapt off the ground, one foot landing on Drago's back as she launched herself upward.

Her hand closed around the glowing blue orb, and power rushed through her. Cassie hit the ground with a smile on her face. Arcs of blue energy ran down her arms, infusing her with a strength she couldn't believe. Cassie ran forward, using her staff like a baseball bat. The running swing hit Drago in the side and sent him flying backward.

Cassie's blows rained down on Drago's unprotected flesh. She heard something break and realized that her staff shattered against the lizard-man's forearm. Getting the staff repaired wouldn't be a big deal, but the weapon's destruction had snapped her out of her battle rage. Looking down at Drago, she realized he was in bad shape. Both his arms were broken, and his ribs were turning black.

Turning her gaze away from Drago, Cassie glared up at the king. "Are you satisfied now, you cheating bastard?"

The crowd grew silent and scrambled off the dome. The ceiling of vines was slowly lifted from the ground. A quick glance to the side showed that her friends' bonds had been cut and they were being herded toward her.

The king appeared at her side. "That was well fought, Champion." He pulled a small token from inside of his belt and pressed it into her palm. "Go forth with the blessings of our people."

Cassie grinned as her quest updated. She'd done it. When they got back to Promethia, she could go to the guildhall and officially update her class and register as an adventurer. Despite the rough start to this quest, things had worked out perfectly.

The smile on her face disappeared as she looked at ShadowLily. The only thing that could have devastated her best friend that much was if something happened to Tim. Cassie ran forward, pulling her into a hug. "Tell me what's going on?"

"Tim's been arrested," ShadowLily said as she choked back tears.

Rounding on JaKobi, Cassie shouted. "What the fuck? We weren't gone that long."

The fire mage held up his hands in surrender. "Jepsom sent the city guard. There wasn't anything we could do."

"I saw them from the inn," Gaston rumbled. "Twenty armed men."

"Well, there has to be a trial or something, right?" Cassie gazed at the two men.

"Not always," Gaston replied uncomfortably.

Cassie smacked him on the chest. "Not helping." She turned toward JaKobi. "Well, wherever the hell he is, we'll break him out."

"That's the thing." JaKobi looked at the ground. "We don't know."

"They can't find him. No one knows where he was taken," ShadowLily replied despondently.

Gaston put an arm around each of the two women and

moved them toward the mouth of the cavern. "Let's not press our hospitality. When we get back to the inn, I'll put the word out. We'll know where he is before dawn."

"Then we get to do a prison break." Cassie grinned. "He'll be back in your arms by noon."

ShadowLily smiled at them and picked up her pace. There was a look of grim determination in her eyes that said, "I will get him back, and there is nothing in the universe that will stop me."

CHAPTER EIGHTEEN

Sleeping in a new place was never easy for Tim.

Trying to get comfortable in prison for the first night was something else altogether. Tim spent most of the night reading the documents Paul had given him. There was a ton of information to review, and he was determined to be ready to strike if he made it out of the prison in time.

Jepsom couldn't win.

Sometime around two AM, he shelved the papers for the last time and leaned his head against the wall. Prison wasn't nearly as rape-centric as he'd been led to believe by late night TV. *Sons of Anarchy* had shone a light on jail that he hadn't needed to see. Although in this case, that could just be the coding. It wouldn't be very good PR if players had too realistic an experience.

The game needed to be tense, not therapy-inducing.

There was no place for a crime like that in the real world, let alone in a game. Thankfully, these developers had decent common sense. While Tim could still get his ass kicked in here, knowing that something else wasn't going to happen to his ass made him feel safe enough to close his eyes.

Tim rested his head against the rough stone wall and wedged himself into the corner. He would be more comfortable lying down, but he'd also be more vulnerable if someone did try to attack him. Slowly, he pushed the thoughts of getting attacked out of his mind and let them wander in a happier direction. Somewhere between dreaming of ShadowLily and a watermelon vodka slide, his mind went blank, and he was dead to the world.

"What in the fuck was that?" Tim rubbed at his eyes, wondering if he'd heard a noise or if he'd simply dreamt it.

A man's wail came again.

Without hesitation, Tim ran toward the noise. He hit a few dead ends, but eventually rounded the corner into what he thought was the right room. The torches in the area had been extinguished so he couldn't see for shit.

Stepping into the hallway, Tim grabbed a torch from the wall just as the awful sound came again. It was a cry he'd expect to hear from a man suffering from delirium or someone stuck in a fever dream. The noise was pure anguish, like the wail a mother makes when she loses a child.

The pain the man must have been in to make those noises pushed Tim into action. He stepped into the room and lifted the torch above his head. As light slowly filled the room, his eyes found two men in the corner. One was lying down, and the other was kneeling over him.

The man kneeling above the other turned to face Tim, shielding his eyes from the light. "Go back to your cell."

Lowering the torch, Tim focused on the man in front of him, trying to make out his features in the flickering light. "Sheriff Hobbs?"

"I said, go back to your cell." The sheriff sneered as he pointed back the way Tim had come. "I'll make sure this prisoner is taken to a healer."

Tim wasn't sure what was going on. There was no reason

for the sheriff to be down here. The man had made the point several times that guards don't mix with prisoners except during chowtime. If John Hobbs was down here to help the man, why had he found him kneeling over the prisoner in the dark? Maybe the man on the ground wasn't just a prisoner, maybe he was a victim.

Oh, shit!

Tim took a step back before he could stop himself. If this man was being attacked by the sheriff, he couldn't just leave. Well, he could, but Tim knew he'd feel like shit if something happened to the man and he could have helped save him. Thankfully, the sheriff gave him just the "in" he needed to stay put.

"You might not remember from our brief introduction, Sheriff Hobbs, but I'm a healer." Tim smiled sheepishly, trying to play the part of polite inmate. "I helped cure a man who was suffering earlier. I'm sure I could do the same now."

The sheriff stood up, his eyes flashing briefly in the torchlight as they narrowed at Tim. "I told you to get out. Are you going to follow my orders, or are we going to have a problem here?"

"You won't get any problems from me, Sheriff." Tim made sure to look as if the very idea was an affront to his character. "No fighting, no stealing, no bullshit."

A growl rumbled from deep inside of Jon Hobbs' throat. He moved so that he was standing between Tim and the man on the ground. "I'm going to count to ten."

Tim paused, keeping the torch aloft so he could see the entire room. "By then, who knows how many inmates could be in here?" He pointed to the body on the ground. "He wasn't exactly quiet."

"I'm fairly confident it's just the three of us." Sheriff Hobbs took a step closer to Tim. "And since you've interrupted my meal, I'm entitled to another."

Meal?

So the good old sheriff was the killer, but how? And why would he do it? There didn't seem to be any logical reason for this kind of behavior to suddenly start. Then Tim remembered what Davros had said. The guard had mentioned that Jon had been acting differently since he'd returned from his trip.

Something must have happened to him on his vacation.

"I'm sure if you're hungry, I could probably scrounge up a few stray potatoes." Tim kept the torch between them. He'd use it as a weapon if he had to, but the last thing he wanted was to hit the sheriff with it, only to find himself stuck in the dark.

"You cheeky little shit." The sheriff took another step toward him. "I'll make *you* my fucking potato."

Tim tried not to laugh as he jabbed the torch toward the sheriff. Make me his potato. Who said shit like that?

His one offensive spell was flameburst. Tim started going through the motions as the sheriff continued backing him into the opposite corner. Something flicked out of the sheriff's mouth. Either he had an abnormally large tongue, or there was another mouth in there, just like in *Alien*.

Fuck this!

Tim finished the movements of his spell and let it go by pointing at the sheriff. Flames erupted from his open palm, engulfing the area in front of him with fire. Jon's clothes burned and his hair was gone, but he didn't scream. Instead, he took another lumbering step forward.

This just keeps getting better and better.

Tim's fingers worked through flameburst again as his lips moved in a silent prayer to the goddess. He didn't know what he was facing down here, only that the good sheriff wasn't a man anymore. He was going to need some help to get out of this alive.

The spell was finished and Tim started to lift his arm, only to find it clamped to his side. The sheriff's fetid breath washed over Tim's face like the smell of garbage left in a hot car. "I'd rather you didn't."

Tim's concentration was broken, and the spell fizzled out.

"See, we can be civil," Jon whispered. "But I am still hungry. It would have been better for both of us if you'd just walked away."

"I'm starting to see that now." Even with death on the line, Tim couldn't stop himself from running his mouth.

Sheriff Hobbs knocked the torch out of his hand before spinning Tim around and slamming him face-first against the wall. "So hungry."

Tim heard a noise like someone retching, followed by a slithering sound. He imagined something sliding out of the sheriff's mouth, getting ready to attach itself to the back of his neck. He was about to become Jon's next meal.

Something wet touched the back of Tim's neck, and his body started to grow numb.

"Did you hear that?" someone called.

"Yeah, I think it came from over here," someone else responded.

The sheriff slammed Tim's head against the wall. "I can't wait to taste you." He took a step back. "Or drain you." He giggled. "I can never remember which is better."

Tim turned to face the sheriff, surprised to see that he looked the same as he had when Tim had met him in his office this afternoon. His burnt hair and skin were back to normal. Jon's clothes were still in tatters, but the rest of him looked perfect.

Footsteps echoed down the hall. Tim flicked his eyes toward the door, knowing that whoever was coming had just saved his ass. When he turned to look back at the sheriff, the man was gone.

Like a fucking ghost.

Bending down to pick up his torch, Tim lofted it above his

head as his gaze spun wildly, searching for any sign of the sheriff. "Why couldn't he just be a normal serial killer?" Tim groused. It wasn't like the man needed a supernatural edge since they were already imprisoned here. All he had to do was isolate a man, and his chance of getting caught was virtually zero.

Baron and Henry came through the doorway and stopped at the sight of Tim. "What's going on here?" Baron asked as Henry went to check on the man on the floor.

Tim wiped away some of the blood running into his eye. The sheriff must have slammed his head against the wall harder than he'd thought. It was funny how fear took the edge off pain, or maybe it was the surge of adrenaline that did it. Now that the shock was wearing off, his head hurt more than he'd like to admit.

A quick cast of healing orb cleared Tim's head. "I heard a noise and came to find out what it was." He looked at the ground, unsure of what to say next. If he told these men the sheriff was here and had somehow disappeared, they'd think he was crazy. "I found him like this."

Baron peered at Tim's head. "Bullshit. You don't get a gash like that just walking around. Either you two fought or you ran into something else."

Tim noted that Baron hadn't said some*one* else. Maybe he could test the waters. "I ran into the sheriff."

Henry looked at him. "Down here? Not bloody likely. That fat bastard hasn't come down here in years."

"If he was here with you, why didn't we see him come out of the room?" Baron asked, lifting his torch to make sure there wasn't anyone else in the room with them.

This was the part of the conversation where he was going to lose them. "He just kind of vanished." Tim shrugged. This was going about as well as could be expected.

"How about you start from the beginning, and don't leave

anything out," Baron suggested as he pulled a small wooden club from behind his back.

Fuck it. If they didn't believe him and it came to a fight, Tim would pull his daggers and do what he had to. He started his story from when he woke up and ended it when they found him in the room. Henry looked skeptical, but Baron looked intrigued.

"Let me see the back of your neck." Baron motioned for Tim to turn around.

Tim felt the man's fingers brush against his neck. He waited to feel the club smash into the back of his skull, but the blow never came. He turned back around to see a disgusted look on Baron's face.

The inmate was rubbing his fingers together, and there was a clear-ish sticky liquid on them. It kind of looked like when someone covered up a big sneeze, only to find their hand covered in webs of unsightly snot.

Baron wiped his fingers on the floor. "At least that part of your story is true." He shook his head in disbelief. "I never would have guessed it was the sheriff. The man's a little odd, but he's never tried to harm us."

Henry looked at the two men. "I'm still not sold. For all we know, this fucker could be making it all up. Maybe he's the one doing this to us."

Tim pointed at his own chest. "All this started before I got here. And if I wanted you all dead, why would I have healed the guy this morning?"

"Be an easy way to gain our trust," Henry snarled as he stared daggers at Tim.

"Easy now, kid." Baron motioned for Henry to relax. "It might not make sense, but he's telling the truth. What we need to do now is decide what we're going to do with this new information."

Tim looked at their expectant faces, realizing they wanted

him to come up with an answer. "The only thing I can think of to keep people safe is for them not to be alone. It was you guys approaching that saved my ass."

"But he left you alive." Henry looked at Tim mistrustfully.

Baron smiled. "Who's going to believe him? Guy had a welt on his head the size of a lemon. Sheriff probably thought we'd do his dirty work for him."

"Let me see what I can do for him, and then we should get some rest." Tim cocked an eyebrow at Baron. "I'm guessing none of these attacks happen during the day."

"No, they don't. Let's get Lenny up, and I'll start spreading the word." Baron joined Tim by Lenny's side.

It was a simple enough thing for Tim to cast cleanse on the man, and Lenny came out of his fevered state almost instantly. He looked around the room, almost as if he couldn't believe his eyes. Tim hit him with a healing orb to make sure he'd be all right, then stood up to leave.

"Find me if there are any issues. Otherwise, I'll meet you back in the vodka room around ten." Tim ducked out the door.

He was lucky Baron was a reasonable man. If the choice had been left up to Henry, Tim would probably be fighting for his life right now. His ability to heal might not have bought him nearly as much leeway as he would have liked.

At least nobody had died since he'd joined the prisoners.

As long as he could keep everyone alive, he had a chance of getting out of this place in one piece. All he wanted was to get back to the inn and fall asleep in ShadowLily's arms. There was something to be said about the simple things in life. When you found someone you couldn't live without, you had to hold onto them and never let go.

Life seemed like it would go on forever, but it was infinitely short.

In his mind, that was what made us such interesting creatures. People lived their whole lives knowing that they were going to die, and yet they gave to each other with such generosity. Sharing one's soul with another was a gift that couldn't be purchased.

He would get out of this and back to ShadowLily. Even death couldn't stop him.

CHAPTER NINETEEN

"Any word?" ShadowLily asked Ernie for what seemed like the hundredth time.

Ernie scowled at her, then seemed to remember that she was on edge and needed to be treated with care. "None of our contacts have reported him being transferred to any of the smaller jails. There are only so many places remaining where he could be. We'll find out soon enough." The innkeeper frowned. "All of the remaining prisons will be almost impossible to infiltrate."

"Then we need access to a lawyer or some way to petition the crown. If Jepsom is behind this, maybe the high priest can stop him." Cassie tried to sound hopeful. "We'll get him back. That asshole can't just do whatever he wants."

Gaston walked into the room and shook his head when they all turned to look at him. "Nothing yet. I've put the word out to see if anybody reported seeing the guards escorting him. If we can figure out which direction they went, we can quickly narrow down the remaining options."

"If Jepsom is behind this, you should probably just pick the worst one and start there," JaKobi muttered and turned his attention back to the book he was reading.

Cassie smacked him on the arm. "Not helpful." She glanced at her bestie, expecting her to look crushed.

"No, he's right." ShadowLily looked around the room. "Jepsom wouldn't just have Tim arrested. He'd want him tucked quietly out of the way." She focused on Ernie. "Is there someplace like that in the city."

Ernie ran a hand through his beard and cast a suspiciously quick look at Gaston. "There is one place."

ShadowLily made a "come on and spill the beans already" gesture.

"They call it 'the Hole.'" Gaston shuddered as he said it. "It's not a very original name, but it's an apt description for the place."

The assassin continued speaking as if he were reliving a traumatic memory. "Only one way in or out. And that's if you make it through the courtyard of armed guards first. Last time I heard, the garrison supported at least forty men. So at the very least, we'd be looking at ten armed men, with thirty in reinforcements only footsteps away."

"How in the fuck are we going to break into that?" Cassie pouted.

"You aren't," said a voice from behind them.

ShadowLily spun, daggers in hand, but paused when she saw a woman in a dress standing there. Her manservant looked like he could cause some trouble, but the lady seemed harmless enough.

"And you are?" ShadowLily tried to keep her voice level, but it might have come across as a little aggressive. She didn't like it when an attractive woman showed up on her turf and started giving orders.

"Lady Briarthorn. Surely you've heard of me." One at a time, she took off her gloves and handed them to her servant. The man also took her coat before the lady glided into the room. She found a chair that looked sufficiently clean and sat with all the grace of a queen.

Ernie and Gaston bowed to her. Cassie just inclined her mug toward the lady before taking another sip. JaKobi was sitting bolt upright. ShadowLily couldn't tell if he knew who Lady Briarthorn was, or if it was her attractive appearance that was garnering the man's full attention.

"Tim's spoken of you." ShadowLily sat across from Lady Briarthorn. She looked the woman over one more time, wondering why Tim forgot to mention she was a stone-cold hottie.

"I should hope so. We've accomplished quite a bit together. He's a rather resourceful young man." Lady Briarthorn gave her a wry smile in a way that said, "See? You don't have anything to be worried about. I'm not interested in your man."

Lucy Briarthorn's look grew more serious. "Thankfully for both of us, the high priest shares my high opinion of Tim, and has tasked me with securing his release."

ShadowLily felt the first genuine smile cross her face since she'd heard about Tim being arrested. "That's great!"

"I have a letter demanding his immediate release, signed by the high priest. Would you care to join me when I go to present it?" Lady Briarthorn watched ShadowLily intently.

"Let's go." ShadowLily moved toward the door. She stopped when she realized no one was following her. "What's the hold-up?"

Lady Briarthorn rose from her chair and turned to face ShadowLily. Her lips were set in a frown. "We can't go until morning. Despite my cajoling, the sheriff has refused to see us until ten."

"By cajoling, she means screaming obscenities at the top of her lungs," her servant quipped.

"Oh, Reggie, I swear I can't take you anywhere." Lady

Briarthorn extended her hand toward ShadowLily. "Should I have a carriage sent, or would you like to meet me there?"

ShadowLily looked at Lady Briarthorn's hand, unsure if she should shake it or give it a kiss. Deciding that kissing her hand might place the wrong kind of boundaries on their relationship, she shook it. "I'll meet you there."

"Then I will see you all tomorrow at ten." She motioned for ShadowLily to follow her to the door. "Tim is handling a time-sensitive issue for us. The high priest is pulling a lot of strings to make this happen. See that Tim comes through on his end of the bargain."

ShadowLily nodded. There wasn't a verbal answer she was ready to give. Until she knew what Tim was up to, she didn't want to commit herself to a course of action. That didn't quite seem to be a threat, but it let her know exactly where they stood.

Tim's get out of jail free card wasn't free.

ShadowLily opened the door for Lady Briarthorn and replied evenly, "See you at ten."

Lady Briarthorn slipped her gloves back on and beamed at her. "Don't take it personally, dear. It's just business." Her eyes twinkled mischievously. "Although Paul does seem a little more worked up than usual."

Lucy stepped outside and climbed into her carriage. She called from the window, "I'll see you in the morning. Don't be late."

As if she'd be late for this. ShadowLily closed the door and turned to face the room. "I don't trust her."

"Never trust the nobility," Gaston retorted. "They'll smile while stabbing you in the back."

"She didn't seem that bad," JaKobi countered with a smile.

"Men," Cassie sighed dramatically. "They'd run headfirst into a wall if it had a picture of boobs on it."

"Don't knock 'em till you've tried them," JaKobi quipped back.

Cassie grabbed her boobs. "Tried 'em." She flipped him off.

"Point taken." JaKobi put his head down and pretended to read his book.

ShadowLily grabbed a beer from the table. "We have to be there before ten tomorrow. Let's just hope Tim's still in one piece when we get there."

Cassie lifted her mug into the air. "To our fearless leader!"

Cheers went up from around the room. ShadowLily hoped Tim knew they would always come for him. That *she* would always come for him.

The tower was bigger than ShadowLily had imagined.

Not that the size of the single tower mattered in relation to the prison. Gaston and Ernie had assured her that the majority of the prison was below their feet. There was one building with a single door that led down into the darkness. If the prisoners somehow made it out of the dungeon, they would exit into the courtyard they were looking at now.

A courtyard surrounded by ten-foot-tall stone walls that was filled to capacity with armed guards.

By the time any rebellion made it out of the courtyard, the city guard would have been notified. The number of men a potential escapee would face would have been insurmountable. The crown would never allow a prison break to happen; it would tarnish their spotless reputation.

Ernie had joked that some of the thieves in the city said the Hole was the safest place in the whole kingdom, even safer than the palace.

In short, without Lady Briarthorn's help or an army, they weren't getting Tim out of prison. Thankfully, the high priest had come through with the help they needed, but there was a cost. Tim was on a quest for the man, something important enough for Paul to exert his will over that of the cardinal.

She didn't like the idea of her man being stuck in the middle of this political cluster fuck. As much as ShadowLily hated to admit it to herself, Malvonis might have the right idea. Getting out of town and keeping out of this shitstorm until it blew over might have been the safest way to go.

Unfortunately for all of them, it seemed Tim was on a quest chain that required him to be here. Maybe he finally got the kill quest, and all of this would be over one way or another. She smiled and thought of how Tim's quests always felt like a classic game. In every game, all the major storylines ended when you killed the big baddie.

Jepsom was definitely a giant fucking baddie.

The bastard might not have green skin or four arms, extra legs, or a really cool weapon, but that didn't make him any less deadly. The scariest part of the entire situation was they had no idea what kind of skills Jepsom actually possessed. All Shadow-Lily knew for certain was that the cardinal wouldn't have made it to where he was inside of the temple's power structure without being able to intimidate people.

Their little group stopped outside of the gate. A few moments later, a black horse pulled a carriage up alongside them, and Lady Briarthorn exited with the grace of a queen. She walked up to the black iron gate and held out her hand. Reginald placed his walking stick in her palm, and she used it to bang on the gate until someone appeared.

"No admittance!" The guard glared at the group.

"I need to speak to Sheriff Hobbs." When the guard didn't respond, Lady Briarthorn continued, "He's expecting me."

The guard turned and shouted, "Hey, Davros, the sheriff say anything about visitors?"

"Only six times during this morning's briefing," Davros

replied, sounding rather annoyed with the man. He waved the guard away from the gate and opened it himself. "Lady Briarthorn, it's my sincere pleasure. Please allow me to show you and your companions to the sheriff's office."

ShadowLily watched the man fawn over Lady Briarthorn and wondered if she'd ever be important enough in the game for people to treat her that way. It must be a crazy feeling to have people know who you are just by seeing you or hearing your name. On top of that, they not only recognized you but also fell all over themselves to give you whatever you wanted.

Must be nice.

It was too bad that kind of fame normally came with responsibilities. You had to make appearances even when you didn't want to. Every time you left the house, it turned into a photo shoot. Maybe it was better not to be so popular. At least you could wear yoga pants at the grocery store without some asshole snapping a picture of you.

Lady Briarthorn could keep the fame. All ShadowLily wanted out of life was to be comfortable. It'd be nice to wake up not having to worry about the future. She didn't need to drive a Ferrari or live on a multimillion-dollar estate. She wanted to be happy and surrounded by people who cared about her.

Sometimes when life was simple, it was perfect.

Their group followed Lady Briarthorn and Davros to the tower and then inside. Before the door closed behind them, ShadowLily noticed men moving to encircle the courtyard. Getting Tim out of here might not be as easy as presenting a letter from the high priest.

If it came down to a fight, there was no way they'd all make it out of here. They'd be better off getting arrested and then leveraging Gaston's lock-picking skills to make a break for it once things settled down. ShadowLily hoped it didn't come down to a fight. Tim and JaKobi hadn't registered as adventurers, and she was pretty sure if Gaston died, he was gone forever.

Now wasn't the time for big setbacks or losing a friend. Right now, they all needed to take large steps toward the future. Being the first to do things and to find new areas or items was the only way to make enough money for all this to be worth it. She wasn't leaving the game with a bigger bill than when she went into it.

Davros motioned to a man sitting at a desk in the main room. "This is Richard. He will be attending to your needs until the sheriff is ready to see you." He bowed. "If you'll excuse me, I have some duties to attend to in the courtyard."

"Thank you for your assistance, Davros." Lady Briarthorn blessed him with a smile that lit up the entire room.

Davros exited the tower, and ShadowLily stood just behind Lady Briarthorn and whispered in her ear, "The men outside looked like they might be preparing for a fight."

Lady Briarthorn inclined her head to indicate she'd heard what ShadowLily had said. "I have a contingency plan in place." She walked forward until she was standing in front of Richard. The man didn't look up as he furiously scratched notes on a sheet of paper.

"We have an appointment to see the sheriff," Lady Briarthorn declared with the icy impatience of the affluent.

Richard finished what he was scribbling and looked up. He did a quick double-take at all of the people standing before him as if they hadn't been announced moments before. "I've prepared our conference room for you to wait in. The sheriff should be returning momentarily."

"If he isn't collecting the man we've come to have released, there will be hell to pay." Lady Briarthorn glared at the clerk with disgust. "Your sheriff is getting on my last nerve as it is."

"You're preaching to the choir," Richard grumbled as he stood up. "Not that I can do anything about it." He motioned for them to follow him toward the only open door in the tower.

"We've got water and food set up in here." He turned to look at the lady and dropped his voice. "Probably best to avoid it, though."

Lady Briarthorn gave him a curt nod. "Thanks for the tip, and do tell the sheriff to hurry. I have other appointments I must keep today."

Richard looked at her and then lowered his head so he was staring at the ground instead. "I'll do my best."

"I'm counting on it." Lady Briarthorn turned toward the rest of the group. "It looks as though we'll be waiting for a bit. Stay away from the food and drink."

"Never trust prison food," Gaston rumbled as he walked into the room and took a seat.

ShadowLily smiled. It was damn good advice. There were always stories on the news about the quality of food in prisons. While she didn't think prisoners deserved organic everything, they did deserve to eat food that wasn't expired.

That was the burden of our legal system.

If you're going to lock people up, you have to take care of them. And while they didn't need TVs and video games, prisoners deserved access to real food and clean water at the very least. Just don't tell that to the people running the for-profit jails. Because if it comes down to serving you green baloney or spending two more cents to get better meat, they were going to save the two cents every time.

Shit, this jail probably didn't even have simple standards. This was the kind of place where when prisoners died, whoever had them arrested let out a sigh of relief. One less problem for the nobility to worry about when one of their accusers bit the dust.

At least back in the real world, they had trials. They might not always be fair, but they had them. Here in *The Etheric Coast*, it seemed like all you needed to make people disappear was a fat stack of gold. Granted, that seemed to be the case in the real world too. How many people aligned themselves with politicians and ended up dead?

More than she could count on both hands.

ShadowLily sat on one of the available chairs. "What do we do now?"

Lady Briarthorn sat and smoothed out the front of her exquisite dress. "We wait."

"I hate waiting," Cassie grumbled.

JaKobi pulled a book out of his robes. "I brought a little something to pass the time. One thing I've learned in life is that when you deal with a government agency, you have to be prepared to wait."

ShadowLily snorted. "But hey, at least we have snacks we can't eat."

Cassie sat down next to her and put an arm around her shoulders. "Don't worry. Loverboy will be back in your arms before you know it."

"And Reginald should be executing the second part of our plan now." Lady Briarthorn grinned. "They aren't going to know what hit them."

The two best friends shared a look and started smiling. ShadowLily couldn't help but think this wasn't a woman you wanted to trifle with. Lady Briarthorn was the kind of woman you wanted on your side when shit went down.

A little bit of the tension ShadowLily had been harboring since arriving at the dungeon melted. Tim was going to be fine, and with the good lady's help, all of them were going to get out of here in one piece. Sometimes having powerful friends wasn't such a bad thing.

CHAPTER TWENTY

"Son of a bitch," Tim muttered as he worked out the kinks in his back.

Who knew sleeping on the floor in a video game could make you feel so rotten? It was like that one time he and Xander had gotten so drunk they'd passed out under some bushes on the way home from a party. It'd taken at least three days for his neck to stop clicking.

Sleeping in weird places was something best left to the extremely young. So it shall be written that any child over the age of fourteen who sleeps on the floor will wake up with at least one limb in agony. Tim laughed at his own joke; sometimes, he cracked himself up.

It wasn't his fault if no one else got it.

Tim did a few of the stretches he'd learned from a yoga instructor he'd had a crush on. He might be shit at yoga, but he had a thing for women in phenomenal shape and tight pants—not that he'd be able to hit on them now.

ShadowLily was an amazing person, not just a great ass in really tight pants. She was the kind of woman you'd give up a kingdom for. There was no way he'd even consider cheating on her. Besides the fact that it would hurt her, he liked his penis attached to his body too much to risk it.

His girl kinda had a thing with knives.

Not that he'd blame her for removing his manhood for straying. There were certain things you don't do. One of them was cheating. Tim liked to think that cheaters always got caught. The radio station by his house used to do a thing called War of the Roses, where the station would call and say the caller had won free flowers and ask where they wanted them delivered. Guess how many guys fell into that trap?

Always try to put yourself in the best position to succeed. Find someone who matches your vibe and be happy. For him, life was all about celebrating the good times with the people he cared about. Sometimes you just had to ride the wave.

Big Richie the surfer taught him that. Guy rode a wave right into the grave, but he went out doing what he loved.

But Tim didn't need to worry about the stresses of marriage or divorce just yet. Things were amazing between him and ShadowLily, and while they were together most nights, they still each had their own place. It was too early to know exactly where their relationship was leading, but all indications said it was somewhere great.

With his back feeling a little better, Tim made his way out of the cell he'd been sleeping in and toward the common room. Today might be a really long day. They needed to come up with the plan to stop the sheriff. He had absolutely no idea how to do it, but he was confident if they all worked together, they could bring him down.

Baron waved Tim over to his table as soon as he entered the room. "I've got a bowl of slop for you."

Tim peered into the bowl, relieved to find out it was only oatmeal. "Looks ok."

"As far as oats in a bowl go, it's not half bad." Baron swirled his spoon through his oatmeal. "But after a few years, it might as well be that stuff I wiped off your neck last night."

Looking into his bowl, Tim rethought how hungry he was. He shoved the bowl back into the center of the table. "Maybe I'll be hungrier later."

Baron laughed. "Better get used to it, boy. I've been here ten years, and the food's always been the same."

Tim couldn't stop the shudder from running through his body. Having to eat oatmeal every morning for the rest of his life sounded horrible. There were so many great breakfast foods. You could have eggs with just about anything, and the same with pancakes or waffles. Then you got into the fun stuff: sausage, ham, English muffins, hollandaise sauce.

The options were endless.

A life of just oatmeal wasn't a life at all. How could they expect a person to survive on such lackluster fair? It reminded Tim of watching *The Matrix*. Keanu woke up on the ship, and his first meal was protein slop. Imagine going from endless possibilities to gruel. Kinda made a guy wish he'd stayed plugged into the power grid.

Food was the one thing that Tim would allow himself to get plugged into the Matrix for. He loved eating. What he hated about being here was that there wasn't a Joe's. He missed being able to go to his favorite spot and order a meal. He'd been going to the diner for years without knowing it was owned by Sierra's dad. His opinion of the food was solely based on his stomach and not the fact that his girlfriend's dad ran it.

If only they had a Joe's in the game.

Tim smiled as he thought about how much he'd taken breakfast for granted. Now that he was in the clink, he saw the error of his ways. If there weren't more important things to be worried about, he might just sit around thinking about food for the rest of the day. Unfortunately, the sheriff had to be dealt with, and time was of the essence.

"Any ideas after our conversation last night?" Tim watched Baron, wondering who he'd have to kill to get a glass of rumpleberry juice.

"Just that we need to keep a better eye on each other. I've spread the word that we're all going to sleep in the common area and that no one should go anywhere alone." Baron looked at his bowl and pushed the half-eaten mess away. "Not that it will do us any good."

"That's simply not true. The sheriff ran or vanished when he heard just the two of you coming. I think if there were enough of us, we could simply overpower him." Tim shrugged. It sounded too easy, so it probably was. It was more likely he just didn't want to be caught. The longer he could keep up the illusion of being sheriff, the safer the creature was.

"While I've never seen anything like what I saw last night, I think cutting his feeding tube off would probably help." He looked at the mushy oatmeal, thinking about the slime that was on his neck. "If we can grab it."

"Sounds like we'll need bait," Baron mused.

"I don't like the sound of that," Henry said as he joined them at the table with his own bowl of soggy oats.

"I don't know, I thought you liked being tickled by big burly men," Baron tossed out casually.

Tim almost burst out laughing, but a quick glance at Henry told him laughing at the man wasn't a great idea. Henry had been dealt a solid burn; Baron had definitely scored a point.

The red spots faded from Henry's cheeks and he smiled. "Who I let tickle me and how I like them to look is none of your business, you old bastard."

Baron just grinned from ear to ear. "Seems like we found our bait. Now we just have to figure out how to deploy him so we make the catch."

"Spoken like a true fisherman." Tim wondered how a fisherman ended up in this hell hole. Although Baron did seem awfully comfortable coming up with a plan to put one of his own at risk. Maybe he was a pirate?

Oh. My. God. Tim was sitting across from an honest to goodness pirate.

One thing they never talked about in pirate movies was how the men survived. Yes, most of the boats had a selection of dry stores and fresh water, but those only lasted so long. For life out at sea, you needed certain skills. A man who was handy with a fishhook and a blade would be a huge bonus.

It wasn't easy to bring his mind back on track, but Tim managed to do it eventually. He was just about to say something clever when the sheriff walked into the room.

Jon Hobbs focused his eyes on his target and scratched his belly. "I'd like a word."

Tim stood up. "Might as well say it in front of everyone. It's not like they are going anywhere." A few of the men laughed, but Tim felt his heart beating faster. He needed as many people around as possible to make sure he wasn't attacked.

"Out!" the sheriff roared.

People found other places to be and quickly. Only Henry and Baron remained behind. They hadn't seen the sheriff last night, but his appearance today sealed their belief in Tim's story. The man who never came into the dungeons was here, and that was all they needed to know.

Tim looked behind the sheriff and noticed that he'd brought two guards with him. The guards appeared to be on edge. Being trapped in prison filled with men who only ate potatoes and oatmeal didn't seem to agree with them. He would have been nervous too. A sword in this small space wasn't going to do you a lot of good if enough men charged you.

The sheriff, on the other hand, looked calm as a cucumber. "Did you not hear what I said?" He pointed at Baron and

Henry. "Get the fuck out of here. I need a word with Tim alone."

"I think we'll stay," Baron replied off-handedly as if he were commenting on the weather. "Our friend here was just telling us the most interesting story."

The sheriff's eyes almost burst out of his head. He focused all his rage on Tim. "Stories are best left for the children at bedtime, don't you think?"

"This was more of a scary story," Tim quipped. "Not suitable for children at all."

"I see." The sheriff's rage melted, replaced by a look of icy indifference. "Nothing to be done about it now. I just hope that these two don't have an accident while you're away."

"While I'm away?" Tim spluttered. The statement didn't make sense. The sheriff wouldn't just let him go, not after what he'd seen. Was the man telling him that he was going to die now? Were Baron and Henry due to meet a similar fate since he told them what happened?

If that was the case, he was going to go down fighting.

Jon Hobbs held up his hands in a disarming manner. "I was thinking about ending this right now, but there is a very persistent bitch upstairs waiting for you, and I believe I've come up with a delicious alternative."

A smile stretched across his face, and he patted his belly. "I'll be seeing the two of you later." Jon pointed at Tim. "Come with me."

The only person Tim knew who was powerful enough to get him out of here was the high priest, probably with assistance from Lady Briarthorn. In the movies, the ladies of this era were all "stab you in the back and simper and preen," but she wasn't anything like that. Tim wouldn't be surprised to find out she could handle herself in a pinch.

Only idiots thought of women as inferior.

Think of how much more we could have accomplished if

women had been allowed to help more throughout history. Some of the country's greatest patriots were women, and most of them did it at a time where women were looked down upon. Imagine the courage it took to run an underground railroad when not being escorted by a man when you left the house was considered too forward.

His friends had come to get Tim just like he thought they would, but they'd come too soon. If he left now, the sheriff was going to take it out on these two men. Tim couldn't let that happen, but he also couldn't stay.

He turned to face Baron and Henry, unsure of what to say. Thinking on the fly, he reached into his inventory and pulled out his daggers. He flipped the blades over and handed them to the men, hopefully without the sheriff seeing. "I'll be back for you."

Baron gave him a sad smile as he tucked the dagger into his shirt. He pulled out a small letter and handed it to Tim. "If and only if I'm not around for some reason, get this to Helen Peters."

"I'll see that you get to deliver it yourself." Tim put the letter in his pocket. He knew what was happening. These men expected to die, and he was pretty sure there was nothing he could do to stop it.

Henry tucked the dagger into his belt. He pulled out a small scrap of parchment and placed it in Tim's hand. "Felix Hardgrove." A tear streaked down his cheek.

"I'll see it done." Tim looked at the two men. "I will be back for you."

Quest Received: Dying Declarations

You've been tasked with delivering two letters upon the deaths of the men who gave them to you. There is no more sacred duty than getting the last words of a loved one to the people they left behind.

There is no reward for this quest, you selfish bastard, it's just the right thing to do.
Accept Quest: Yes/No
Tim accepted the quest.

Tim had meant what he'd said to them. If anything happened to these men, he'd make sure their letters were delivered.

It wasn't that Tim was driven by some bond of brotherhood that formed miraculously after one night. In fact, he kind of disliked Henry. The thing that bothered him was that these men were in danger because of him, and he hated knowing that his actions would lead to their deaths. Sure, the sheriff might have killed them eventually anyway, but he'd helped speed up the process.

The sheriff had to be stopped, but now that he was being set free, Tim had no idea how to make that happen.

"Hurry it up, lovebirds, I doubt the cunt upstairs is waiting patiently. Women tend to overreact to delays." Jon Hobbs huffed with impatience.

Tim shook Baron's hand. "Stay safe."

"I'll do my best." Baron poked Tim in the chest with a finger. "You just follow my instructions."

Henry grinned and slapped Baron on the chest. "Guess I was wrong about him."

"Holy shit, Henry just admitted he was wrong. Now I can die a happy man." Baron wrapped an arm around Henry's shoulders. "Let's get out of here before the sheriff loses his patience."

Tim turned away from the two men to face the smug-faced bastard in front of him. "Lead the way."

The two guards looked relieved as they scurried toward the door like cockroaches trying to avoid the light. The sheriff followed them. Despite his implied impatience, the sheriff seemed happy enough to take his time getting out of the dungeon.

Jon Hobbs' belly rumbled. "As soon as we get this business taken care of, I'm going to need a snack."

Tim shuddered, thinking about what it would feel like to be drained by the man in front of him. He'd seen the after-effects and heard the screams that accompanied a feeding. By all accounts, it was something he never wanted to experience. His gut twisted as he thought about all the men trapped down here with this monster in their midst.

He'd find a way to kill the bastard.

CHAPTER TWENTY-ONE

Jon Hobbs walked into the conference room with the swagger of a Greek god.

Tim couldn't believe that with everything going on, the man felt so confident. Everyone in this room would know his secret soon enough, and then the jig would be up, not to mention the quest Tim had taken to stop him. There was no way he was letting this drop, not when Baron's and Henry's lives hung in the balance.

The sheriff couldn't be allowed to continue feeding on the inmates. Part of Tim wondered if whatever had come back over the mountain could even be considered Jon Hobbs any more. It almost felt like an *Invasion of the Body Snatchers* type thing. Or even worse, maybe it was more of a *The Thing* scenario.

In which case, the entire kingdom might be fucked.

None of that mattered when his eyes locked onto Shadow-Lily. Tim rushed forward, slamming into her hard enough that they crashed to the ground in a tangle of limbs. It'd only been a day since he'd seen her, but it felt like a lifetime apart. When their lips met, he wanted to stay on that spot of the floor forever.

A very polite cough from above them brought Tim back to his senses.

After disentangling himself from the half-elf, Tim smiled at the rest of the collected individuals. "It's good to see all of you."

Lady Briarthorn inclined her head to the sheriff. "I see that you've honored the high priest's request. Was there a reason we had to wait so long?"

Jon Hobbs leaned back in his chair like a man sipping tea on the front porch. "Oh, these things take time. I also needed to have a private word with the inmate."

"We should have done this last night," Lady Briarthorn fumed.

The sheriff glanced at Tim. "You know, I was just thinking the same thing." He waved away the inquiring looks from the people in the room. "I've concluded the prisoner's exit interview. You're all free to go."

Lady Briarthorn's cheeks burned at being dismissed, but she forced a smile onto her face. "Then we shall do so at once." She motioned for everyone to stand.

Tim waited for the room to clear before staring at the sheriff like Clint Eastwood had done in every film he'd ever made. "This isn't over."

The sheriff leaned forward, placed his elbows on the table and rested his chin on top of his folded hands. "I'd forget everything you saw. You're out, and the men imprisoned here don't deserve your pity. Go and live your life. Let this place be nothing but a dark memory."

He could easily walk out of the room and try the old "out of sight, out of mind" trick.

Unfortunately for Tim, that little mind game had never really worked for him. When there was a problem, his brain gnawed at it relentlessly until he fixed it. He couldn't count the number of nights he'd woken up from a dream about something he was wrestling with. Normally it was something from one of his classes, but every now and then, it was a videogame that kept him up until the first rays of dawn touched the horizon.

You had got it bad when you woke up thinking about the best way to tackle a boss.

The sheriff felt like the kind of problem that would keep Tim up at night until he resolved it. It was mostly because he couldn't deal with him right now. There was nothing he hated more than leaving quests unresolved. It was the kind of thing that came back to bite you.

There was no way he would let what was happening in the dungeon continue. While Tim didn't know what the men in the prison were guilty of, he *was* sure they didn't deserve to be snacks.

"I'll be seeing you," Tim replied as he tipped an imaginary cap to the sheriff. "My guess is it will be sooner than you would like."

Jon Hobbs leaned back into his chair again, a genuine smile on his face. "I'm looking forward to it."

The smug fucker thought he could take Tim in a fight just because he was a healer. Jon would learn the hard way that a monster who faced off with the Blue Dagger Society rarely lived to wreak havoc again. In fact, he couldn't think of one monster who'd escaped death once the guild set their sights on it.

Part of him wanted to say something else, but Lady Briarthorn was waiting at the exit of the tower, and she looked impatient. Tim tapped his hand on the stone and walked out of the room to catch up with the rest of the group.

Just outside the tower, Lucy Briarthorn stopped him. "I'm

sorry it took me so long to secure your release." She looked genuinely worried. "Do you have everything you need for tomorrow?"

Tim had formed a rudimentary plan, but there wasn't anything set in stone. Some of what he planned on doing depended on who was in the stands and how Jepsom responded to their initial attack.

"I think I'm good." Tim reached out to shake her hand. "Thanks for getting me out of here."

Lucy gave Tim's hand a firm squeeze. "If you come through for us tomorrow, it will have been well worth the effort. I'll let you see to your final preparations. Have a good day." She dropped his hand and walked to the exit.

Davros caught up to him just before he reached the others. "Sorry about the…" He paused and mimicked punching Tim in the stomach. "No hard feelings, I hope."

Tim was pissed at first, but maybe there was a way he could use this man. "The sheriff isn't what he seems. The prisoners are in danger."

"What do you want me to do about it?" Davros moved a few steps away from Tim as if standing too close to him might get him in trouble.

"Just keep your eyes open, I might need your help when I come back." Tim went to shake his hand but stopped himself. He was sure there was more than one pair of eyes on them.

"No one ever comes back." Davros gave Tim a lopsided grin. "But then again, no one has ever left before." He leaned close before whispering, "If you come back, I'll help you."

Tim couldn't have his inside man watched too closely, but at least he could get a little payback. He took a swing at Davros. His fist connected with the man's stomach. "Fuck you, too."

He leaned over the winded man like he was going to mock him and whispered, "Be ready."

Lady Briarthorn's carriage was already rolling as the gates closed behind them. The rest of the guild formed a half-circle around him. Tim could tell by the looks on their faces they were genuinely happy to see him.

Cassie poked him in the chest. "You had us worried, asshole."

Tim held up his hands. "Not a lot I could do about it. I'm just happy you weren't there when they came for me." Tim looked from his fiery little tank to the woman of his dreams. "Where were you two, anyway?"

ShadowLily wrapped her arm in Tim's and started pulling him toward the inn. "It's a long walk back. How about we fill you in on our adventure, and then you can tell us what's next?"

"Well, about that..." Tim stopped as ShadowLily put a finger to his lips.

"Our story first," the half-elf purred into his ear.

"And it's crazy. There was a giant lizard, and Cassie kicked its ass." JaKobi doubled over as Cassie punched him in the gut.

Tim chuckled. There seemed to be a lot of stomach-punching going around.

"It's better when I tell it." Cassie brushed some imaginary dirt from her shoulder. "Now that I'm an adventurer."

"Congrats." Tim was excited. Half his party had taken the plunge. It was making his choice easier to see how excited they all were about the opportunity.

"Now listen closely because I'm only going to tell the story once." Cassie paused. "Who am I kidding? You're going to hear it like a million times. So there we were..."

Tim started to tune her out when ShadowLily leaned her head against his shoulder. "It's actually a good story the first time. On listen number fifteen, I started to find it lacking."

He pulled her close and kept walking toward the inn. He felt so comfortable here with his friends that he never wanted to leave. Back in the real world, there were no more dragons to slay or things to conquer, but in *The Etheric Coast,* there were infinite possibilities. Life in the game was whatever you wanted to make it.

People were going to be talking about what he created for years.

It felt so good to step into the inn.

The Blue Dagger felt like home. You know that feeling when you catch a scent and it gives you a huge hit of nostalgia. That was how Tim felt right now. Who knew the smell of stale beer and sawdust would make him feel so comfortable.

All it took was one night in a dungeon to make his little room look like a palace, and there was beer. Potato vodka was okay stuff, but beer was where his heart was. Plus, he could drink a few of them and drive. If he hit the hard stuff, he had to call a ride. One thing he never did was drive when he was drunk.

If Tim went out for a night on the town with the intention of drinking more than a few, he took a cab. The twenty bucks it cost to get from campus to the bars was worth it. He could get drunk with his buddies and not even be tempted to drive. Or if they were at home, you could have just about anything delivered. Why risk hurting someone else or yourself when Taco Bell was only a few clicks away from your door.

The inn didn't have an app, but it had a Liz.

The woman he'd helped out of her previous job had a beer in his hand before he was five steps inside. "Welcome back."

Ernie came out of the kitchen with a tray of food. "I thought you might be hungry." The innkeeper pulled a letter out of his pocket. "Mr. Applebottom left this for you."

He had a beer and potentially good news in his hands. Now

all he had to do was figure out a way to get rid of the sheriff and Jepsom. This was a problem that he ran into a lot. He loved the storylines of quests so much he always took on way too many of them. To be fair, Tim thought he'd be in the dungeon for a few days, but things hadn't worked out that way.

ShadowLily dragged him toward a table. "Do you really think your plan for tomorrow will work?"

"I don't know. The only thing we can do is go for it." Tim took a sip of his beer.

JaKobi grinned after taking a sip from his own mug. "Kicking ass and taking names."

"Distraction duty isn't fit for the Destroyer of Lizards." Cassie gazed into her beer as if it would reveal the world's greatest unsolved mysteries.

"Trying out new nicknames for yourself?" Tim snorted. "Is distraction duty good enough for the Lady Who Talks too Much?"

Cassie picked up something from the food tray and threw it at him. "It's a good thing you just got out of prison, asshole."

Tim grinned at her as he started making a plate of food. "I get the feeling this is supposed to be a *mano a mano* fight. My final test before making the first-class change."

"Seems dangerous is all," Cassie replied before starting to put together her own plate of food.

"Like a cage match with a giant ass lizard wasn't?" JaKobi stood up, grinning like a mad man. "You should have seen her, Tim. I would have been shitting myself trying to run away, but Cassie went toe to toe with that monster."

"A man who can shit and run at the same time has many talents." Gaston nudged JaKobi. "Read that on a bathroom stall once."

The fire mage nodded. "Sage advice, my friend, sage advice."

Tim looked around the room and thought about how much fun he was having. Sure there was always tomorrow's fight looming over his head. It was stressful, but knowing that he had these awesome people in his life made it so much better. When the shit hit the fan, his entire guild came running. That was the kind of support money couldn't buy.

The bonds of friendship could be stronger than Gandalf facing down a Balrog.

CHAPTER TWENTY-TWO

Tim pushed his bowl of oatmeal away.

The meal reminded him too much of the last one he'd shared with Baron and Henry. Thankfully he had a giant glass of rumpleberry juice and a plate of bacon.

Wasn't life always better with bacon?

Smiling to himself as the salty meat melted in his mouth, Tim looked over his team. Each of them looked calm. Why shouldn't they be? They had conquered every task they'd ever taken on. If he had to be honest with himself, the Blue Dagger Society was pretty badass.

Still, there was that tiny bit of worry worming its way into his skull. Deep down, Tim was a worrier at heart. He liked to have a plan and several backup plans in place for different scenarios that might derail his original options. He didn't like to go into a fight unless there was a possibility of controlling all the variables. He knew all the logistics of today's ceremony.

So he should have felt confident.

Instead, Tim felt worried. There were so many things that could go wrong. If the fight raged out of control, innocent people in the crowd could be hurt. That's why his plan revolved around getting as many people away from the ceremony before his attack as possible.

The only way he'd stand a chance to win was if he didn't have to worry about the crowd. They might just be NPCs, but killing innocent bystanders wasn't something he wanted to do. At least Gaston had been able to replace the daggers he'd given away, so Tim had something he could use to try to kill that bastard Jepsom. Otherwise, he'd have to rely on flameburst, and while he'd dedicated some time to leveling the spell, it wouldn't be the thing that tipped the scales against the cardinal.

Tim wanted this fight to be up close and personal.

He was ready to kill the fucker. Jepsom had gone out of his way to make Tim's life harder just because he'd taken the time to heal a peasant who couldn't afford the temple's services. They say no good deed goes unpunished, and sometimes it was true, but fuck those people.

Tim wasn't going to stop helping others just because people wanted him to stop.

There was a feeling that he got when he selflessly helped someone. You never know what a person's going through; doing something small like covering a dollar when they were short at the register could make all the difference in their lives. A small bit of kindness could be all it takes to make someone's day.

Polishing off the rest of his juice, Tim leaned against ShadowLily, his mind already jumping to the business of the day. "Ready to go?"

She winked at him. "As long as you are." She grabbed Tim's chin and forced him to look her in the eye. "We're all going to be there for you. So get out of your own way and just do your thing."

Cassie placed a hand on Tim's shoulder. "We've got this."

"What she said." JaKobi grinned at them as he shoved the last three pieces of bacon in his mouth at once.

Gaston twirled one of his daggers on a fingertip. "The real question is, why don't you want us to do more?"

Tim couldn't put his finger on it. There was no rule that said he had to fight Jepsom alone, but he'd learned to trust his instincts a long time ago. He might be overly cautious, but he was rarely surprised. He was also prudent and didn't want to lose because of his pride.

"Oh, I'm counting on all of you to bail my ass out of the fire when the shit hits the fan. They say no plan survives first contact with the enemy. So if you see Jepsom get the upper hand, feel free to help out." Tim looked around at their smiling faces.

"So much for doing this alone," Cassie chided.

"My pride can take the hit of having help, but not of letting him win." Tim grinned. "So don't wait too long if I'm in trouble." He stood and walked toward the door. "Let's go."

Once their group made it out of the slums, they headed in the direction of the temple. Outside of the massive building, there would be a stage set up and some seating erected for those too wealthy to stand with the huddled masses and one lowly assassin with friends in high places.

The high priest would give a speech, and Jepsom would accept his reward before giving a speech of his own. It was during his speech that Tim planned to make his move. Lady Briarthorn had arranged for him to have a seat in the front row, virtually guaranteeing him access to the cardinal.

As they reached the temple steps, the group split up. Their plan hinged on them not being noticed together. Anyone traveling with Tim could be marked by Jepsom's people and someone might remember a group of five coming to the event together if there was an attack.

And there was going to be an attack of epic proportions.

Jepsom and his reign of terror were going down. Who knew how many lives that bastard ruined by refusing to heal people. Imagine having the ability to cure any disease, to mend any broken bone, and then denying access to the people who needed those treatments. No one should have to die so someone could turn a profit.

He wished there was more magic in the real world. Too many great people died of cancer. That shit was the king of all motherfuckers. Ryan Reynolds had said it best when he'd simply stated, "Fuck Cancer!" If the choice was to heal what he could or be called a criminal, Tim was going to keep healing.

They had called Rick Simpson a criminal too.

Now he was the hero of a revolution. Tim might not believe you could kill cancer with cannabis alone, but he'd seen too much evidence suggesting it helped to ignore it. If he ever got the Big C, he'd be taking his normal treatments and as much pot as he could handle. If the choice was death or eating a bunch of Rick Simpson Oil, he'd get a penchant for edibles real quick.

It was the logical choice.

Thankfully for him, the cardinal wasn't something he had to fight a long, agonizing battle with. Whatever happened between them would be settled today. Jepsom was a tumor that had latched itself onto the temple, and he needed to be cut out. Once the cardinal had been removed, Paul could run the temple in a way that benefited all the citizens of Promethia.

When you were a healer, you cared about more than just billing or selling certain medications for kickbacks. Wanting to help people live their best and longest lives was a calling. Not everyone was made for it. That was why when people found a doctor who really cared about them, they would stay their patient forever.

Finding someone who cared about your health as much as you did wasn't easy.

That was why Tim tried to spend a little time with each of his patients instead of just throwing a *Healing Orb* at them and taking their money. Part of the process was healing their minds from whatever incident had occurred.

Having a broken arm one instant and a fully functional one the next, wasn't something everyone was used to. Imagine having the mental trauma from a major accident but your body was fine. It took folks time to process their recovery, and he was there to help them with that as well.

With the high priest's and Lady Briarthorn's help, Tim could offer those types of services. Shit, even Ironbeard had given him extra time to focus on his healing. Everything was working out perfectly.

Not to mention his plan to buy out the buildings next to the inn. In his inventory, he held a signed letter for the properties. As long as he had the gold in the account within five days, he'd be the proud owner of every single building he wanted. He didn't know how Applebottom had secured them all, but it always paid to hire the best people for the job.

Sometimes the best cost a little more, but savings in peace of mind were not measurable.

Tim moved through the crowd until he found his seat in front of the raised stage. He sat down and waited for the ceremony to start. It wouldn't be long now until his future inside of *The Etheric Coast* was decided. He'd either kill Jepsom and move on or die trying. There wasn't room for any middle ground.

He fanned himself with the program for the event and casually looked around. He spotted JaKobi and Cassie but not his thief or assassin. Granted, if they were easy to spot, they wouldn't be very good at their jobs. Tim trusted that they were in the right positions and everything was in place.

The next few hours would decide his future, and Tim was ready to embrace the challenge.

CHAPTER TWENTY-THREE

The crowd quieted as the high priest took the stage.

Paul stepped up to a small podium and looked over the grouping. "The goddess is truly blessed to have so many dedicated followers. Using her light to guide us, we must all strive to be the best versions of ourselves. To truly embrace the divine, one must be not only devoted but compassionate and charitable."

After another review of the masses, the high priest continued, "Let the words of the goddess direct you in all things. Her teachings serve us all. Her words fill us with hope for the future."

Glancing toward the men seated on the stage, Paul motioned to Jepsom. "We've come together today to honor one man who exemplifies the will of the goddess, our very own Cardinal Jepsom."

Jepsom inclined his head to the high priest and offered him the slightest of nods.

Paul smiled warmly as he turned back to face the crowd. "Today, we honor the cardinal for a job well done. With his guidance, our temple has truly become the envy of the continent. Every high priest around the realm is trying to recruit him into their service."

He slammed a fist on the podium. "But I said no! The cardinal is too valuable of a resource for us to part with. The people of Promethia deserve the best."

"Thus, we celebrate the man who thinks of others before himself in every situation. Who would give the very last coin in his purse to help someone in need. A man who would do anything to better the lives of friend and foe alike."

Paul paused for dramatic effect. "I present to you the newly minted Cardinal of the Seven Seals." The high priest started clapping, and the cheering crowd swallowed up whatever was said between the two men before Jepsom claimed the podium.

A smug smile twisted the cardinal's lips almost into a sneer. He looked directly at Tim before turning to face the adoring masses. Tim looked at where the cardinal had been sitting and was shocked to see the high priest sitting next to Jon Hobbs.

Lifting a hand to silence the crowd, Jepsom started to address the gathered masses. "In the spirit of giving, a good friend of mine has asked that I preside over the funeral of two local inmates. I thought it would be appropriate to welcome these men back into the goddess' embrace before thanking you all for this glorious position."

Jepsom's smile turned warm and caring, something Tim wasn't sure the man was able to accomplish until that very moment.

Two caskets were carried onto the stage. Tim felt a sinking sensation in his gut. The sheriff was here, and there were only two other men who knew his secret. Were Henry and Baron in those coffins? He looked away from the two white boxes and back up at the podium. The cardinal winked at him before scanning the crowd with a sorrowful expression on his face.

"The goddess' light shines upon us all. In her eyes, no man is worth more than any other," Jepsom said with just the right trace of self-deprecation.

Tim snorted in disbelief. The cardinal was the kind of man who'd have your throat slit for scuffing his boots, and he was up there giving a speech about equality. It made him fucking sick.

"These two men might have died in prison, but their light will move on. All of us deserve the chance at redemption." The cardinal paused. He let the tension build for a moment and then continued, "Baron Peters and Henry Hardgrove, I welcome you into the goddess' embrace. May your souls find the happiness in death that they never found in life."

Jepsom lifted his hands into the air, and a beam of brilliant white light shot into the heavens. "The goddess has welcomed them with open arms." The cardinal looked down at Tim with a smile pulled tight across his face before returning his gaze to the admiring crowd. "It is times like this, my friends, that my duties as cardinal fill me with happiness, but there are other times my duties are not so welcome."

The crowd gave a gasp of horror. All of them were eating up this lunatic's bullshit. Tim had heard enough. He took a red cloth from his robes and held it in the air. The little bit of fabric rippled as if on a breeze as he waved it a few times before letting it drop to the ground.

Cassie screamed, "Jepsom is a fraud! Don't listen to his bullshit."

The guards by the stage started running toward Tim's master of distraction. Tim leaned forward in anticipation of the next part of his plan unfolding. He really hadn't expected this part to work, but there was always the chance they would take him by surprise. His eyes moved from the guard's back toward the podium, and he held his breath.

The world around him froze. It was like one of those scenes from *Saved By the Bell* where the main character paused everyone so he could monologue to the camera. "What the fuck?" Tim exclaimed as he looked around for the source of the spell.

A woman appeared out of nowhere and started walking through the crowd in Tim's direction. Her robes were blue, but glowed with a white light. "Not how I'm used to being addressed." The goddess smiled. "But I think I can let it slide under the circumstances."

The goddess seemed a lot hipper than she had the last time he had interacted with her. Tim wondered if the AI who ran *The Etheric Coast* was learning from its interactions with the players and tailoring the game experience to each of them. It would have to be amazingly sophisticated software, but who would want to leave a game where everything seemed made just for them?

Tim wasn't sure if he should stand or bow, so he just remained seated. "Sorry." He winced. Sorry wasn't the kind of thing you said to a goddess. He should have said something like "Please forgive me, your divine worship."

"Yes, that would have been better." The goddess stopped in front of him.

Holy shit, did she just read my mind?

"Yes, but I don't have enough time to explain things now. I'm here to cash in on the favor you owe me." Her eyes said, "Just nod your head so I can give you the details."

There was no way he could deny the goddess. Whatever she wanted him to do, he had to do it. She'd saved Cassie's life, and the only reason he was able to put his plan for the slums in place was because of his work with the temple.

Tim looked into the goddess' expectant eyes and spoke with true eloquence. "Okay." Sometimes he wasn't so great with words under pressure, and he had no idea what else the goddess might want from him. He was already here doing what the high priest had asked him to.

"You can't kill the cardinal," the goddess tried to continue, but Tim cut her off.

"No fucking way." He was pissed. Jepsom had made his life teeter on the edge of miserable since he'd come into the game. If he didn't have such awesome friends, he would not have wanted to stay.

The goddess' eyes blazed with fury but her voice was calm. "You owe me this. It might not make sense now, but all things will become clear in time." Her light started to fade, and the sounds of the world around him started to return. "The choice is yours."

Things were speeding up now. What in the fuck was he going to do? Tim knew he only had seconds to make the decision. The goddess had never steered him wrong. His future, like it or not, was tied to her in ways he couldn't fathom.

"Fuck," he growled. Was he really about to save Jepsom's life?

Jumping up from his seat, Tim pointed to where he thought Gaston might be standing. "Look out!"

When Jepsom saw Tim stand up, he activated the dungeon heart's power and his personal shield erupted around him. The daggers that had been aimed at his back bounced harmlessly away. He stared at the young man and wondered why he had given everything away a moment before he could have taken his revenge.

There was no way Paul would be able to pry the kid from his clutches this time, not after an open attempt on the cardinal's life in such a public place. Tim was going to be punished for picking the wrong side, but not before he murdered that old fool Paul. This was his moment; soon he would be High Priest Jepsom the Great.

He added that last part to the title, but people would remember his name for generations. How could the masses not? He was going to be the greatest high priest who ever lived.

Smiling, Cardinal Jepsom stood tall and looked at Tim with a self-satisfied expression. "There won't be a next time."

The words echoed through his head like a migraine.

Tim looked at the cardinal. He already knew it was true. This had been his one chance to end things, and he failed. Not only had he failed, but he'd been duped into doing it by the goddess. His most likely reward for honoring his promise?

An early death.

Fuck.

Sometimes life was a cold, hard bitch. Tim glared at the cardinal's smug face and flipped him the bird. It was a childish gesture, but it made him feel a million times better. He wasn't going to die letting that asshole think Tim cared about him.

Something landed at his feet, and Tim looked down to find a tiny leather-bound book. White light shone around the edges. Bending down, he picked up the book and opened it. There was an inscription on the first page.

For honoring your promise.

Tim flipped to the next page and saw that this was another spell book. There were two spells listed. He was about to learn how to cast weaken undead and divine light. The second spell looked like some kind of attack spell.

Tim's jaw dropped. He'd be learning both spells at the apprentice level right off the bat. He might be about to die, but he couldn't fault the goddess for providing awesome rewards, even if they wouldn't last for long.

Then it hit him.

Why would the goddess give him this awesome reward if

she was going to let him die? You didn't do this kind of thing for someone unless you expected them to live. Maybe he still had a chance.

Tim looked at the stage and took a quick step back. He would have taken another step, but he'd already backed into his chair. His eyes were no longer on Jepsom but firmly focused on the two caskets next to him. Their lids were off, and there was something moving inside the boxes.

What in the fuck was going on?

CHAPTER TWENTY-FOUR

Baron leapt out of his casket.

At least Tim thought it was Baron. The man was the right size, but it was hard to tell with his jaw gaping and some kind of serpentine tube sticking out of it. There were teeth on the end of that thing, and they snapped open and closed.

Tim tried to calm his nerves and thought about the new spells he'd just been given. Seemed like they would be a complete waste if they weren't made for this situation. He started working on the movements for weaken undead. When he glanced to see how long he had before Baron attacked him, he found the monster version of his friend going after Jepsom.

Henry joined Baron a moment later, and the two creatures started slamming themselves against the cardinal's shield. Despite the strength the two monsters had, they couldn't get in. Then a third man landed on top of Jepsom's shield, and it started to buckle. The sheriff had decided to join the party.

Tim wondered what could possibly be driving these creatures to attack Jepsom in the open. This seemed like a "the jig is up" move for the sheriff. There was no putting the cat back in the bag after you landed on top of the cardinal with some kind of crazy vampiric feeding tube coming out of your kisser."

Something bumped into his shoulder, and Tim whirled. ShadowLily and Gaston joined him, and he could see Cassie and JaKobi working their way through the screaming crowd.

"I had the perfect throw," Gaston lamented.

Tim put a consoling hand on his shoulder. "I'm sure you did, and I wouldn't have interfered with a master at work if the goddess herself hadn't asked me to."

Gaston seemed mollified, but Tim could already see the wheels in his head spinning with questions. "Let's talk after we take care of our current problem." He pointed at the three creatures trying to crack Jepsom out of his shield like a walnut at a Christmas party.

"What problem?" Cassie huffed. "Those guys are doing the job for us."

It took a second for it to click, but then all the pieces fell into place for Tim. He pulled his bewildered tank into a hug. "You beautiful bastard!"

Tim let go of his perplexed friend and looked at the entire group. "Our job as I see it now is to get these people out of here so we can deal with the three creatures."

"Any chance we can wait until they kill him to help?" JaKobi shrugged when they all glared at him. "I'm just saying. Jepsom doesn't seem like the kind of guy who'd stop trying to kill you because you saved his life."

JaKobi was right, but Tim wasn't sure if that was what the goddess would want. Fuck, when he tried to think about what an actual god might want he had no idea. A god's thoughts and desires might not be comprehensible to a mere mortal.

Fuck it. He was just going to have to do what he thought was right. "No, we go now. We'll deal with Jepsom later. He just told everyone the sheriff was his friend, and the man's up there trying to eat him. Jepsom's going to have plenty of explaining to do."

"Not that it matters now." Cassie pointed at the stage.

ShadowLily snickered. "That's gotta hurt."

The cardinal's shield had finally collapsed, and the sheriff was crouched over him, trying to fend off the other two creatures. It seemed Jon Hobbs wasn't the kind of monster who liked sharing with his friends. It wouldn't be much longer before the other two creatures gave up and started looking for other sustenance.

Tim grabbed Cassie by the shoulder. "Use that big scary voice of yours to get these people to scatter."

Tim turned to the rest of the group and continued, "I've got a spell that can weaken them and one that should harm them, but I can't use them at the same time. That means the three of you have to distract the other one until I'm ready to deal with it."

"What about the big fucker guarding Jepsom?" JaKobi asked.

"We'll let Jepson and the sheriff work out their differences until we take care of the other two," Tim replied with a smile. It wasn't his job to keep saving the bastard's life. At least he hoped it wasn't.

Cassie jumped up on the stage. "Get the fuck out of here!" It wasn't eloquent, but she got the point across. Then she pointed at a guard. "Once these people are out of here, set a perimeter. None of these things can leave."

The guard stared at her blankly. The man was clearly in shock. No one expected monsters to show up while they were just trying to pick up a little bonus pay.

Cassie slapped the guard across the face, breaking the man out of his stupor. "Get to fucking work."

The guard took control of his men and formed a wall to push the crowd away from what was happening on stage.

The sheriff won his battle of dominance over the prize, and

Baron and Henry turned away, looking for easier snacks. Tim fumbled through the motions of weaken undead. As he finished the spell, he muttered. "I'm sorry I couldn't help you."

Tim let the spell go, and it hit Baron squarely in the chest. With Baron weakened, Tim started casting divine light. He hoped the spell would be painless for the man, or rather, for the creature that he'd become. He'd promised these prisoners he would deliver letters to their loved ones if they died. Part of him hoped he'd be able to return the letters to them instead of letting them down the way he had.

Putting an end to the sheriff would go a good long way toward easing his guilt.

Tim finished casting divine light, and a cone of pure power darted from his fingertip at Baron. The creature tried to duck out of the way, but the spell hit him in the center of the chest. White flames erupted from where the spell landed and consumed Baron in a single white-hot flash.

Cassie was going toe to toe with the creature formerly known as Henry. Her bō staff was long enough that Henry couldn't quite reach her with his fancy new mouth. Gaston and ShadowLily worked with her, trying to corral and attack the creature at the same time. Tim could see several cuts along Henry's arms and legs. The wounds didn't seem to be slowing the creature down at all.

Tim remembered how infective his *flameburst* had been. The sheriff had repaired the damage almost instantaneously.

Henry erupted in flames as JaKobi entered the fray. Everyone moved away from the flaming creature except for Tim. He kept marching forward. He blasted the creature with *Weaken Undead* and then with *Divine Light*. Henry ceased to exist an instant later.

That left Tim with one last target to destroy.

The sheriff climbed off Jepsom's corpse and roared. Something was going on. Jon Hobbs' clothes ripped at the seams as his arms and legs elongated. It was like he'd turned into the Hulk. Whatever Jepsom had been using to power his shield had drawn the monster toward him, and it seemed the sheriff had absorbed that power.

"Boss fight!" Tim shouted to the rest of his group.

This was going to be fucking awesome!

The sheriff picked up Jepsom's corpse and turned slowly until his eyes locked onto Tim's. The crazy feeding tube sucked back into his mouth. "I told you this wasn't over." He let out a roar and his mouth split open so the snapping jaws of his second mouth could terrify them all.

With the casual flick of his wrist, the sheriff sent Jepsom's body sailing at them.

JaKobi stepped forward, casting flameshield. Jepsom's body flew through the fiery construct and came out as ashes on the other side. JaKobi's spell winked out of existence, and the sheriff sprinted toward them.

Cassie charged forward to intercept the gigantic version of Jon Hobbs. "Asshole!" she screamed as she smashed her bō staff into his leg.

Hobbs shrugged off her attack and shoved Cassie out of the way as he continued toward Tim.

JaKobi hit the sheriff with spell after spell. Jon Hobbs' torso looked like a burnt pincushion. The hilts of twenty throwing knives littered the sheriff's chest like popcorn on the floor of a movie theater. Cassie leapt to her feet and ran forward, striking the sheriff from behind. Jon Hobbs ignored her.

The man was a juggernaut.

Tim cast weaken undead, then he cast it again. The spells were enough to slow the sheriff down, but the third stopped him in his tracks. Using the last of his mana, Tim cast divine light.

The shimmering projectile caught Jon Hobbs in the center of the chest, and he screamed as the fire consumed him. Flakes of his skin floated away on the breeze. After three seconds, all that was left of the sheriff was a bad memory.

Darkness spread across the sky, and a bolt of red energy shot out of the roiling black clouds. The bolt struck the front of the temple and seared an angry red mark on the central pillar.

A voice called from the heavens, "We are hungry, and we are coming for you all."

White light erupted from the temple, banishing the darkness from the sky in an instant. The light gathered in on itself, and the goddess was once again standing before Tim. "The Dark Lord Vitaria has awoken. Will you be my champion in the fight against her darkness?"

Tim looked at his team. One by one, they nodded, letting him know they were all on board with the decision.

Turning to face the goddess again, Tim dropped to one knee. "I will be your champion."

The goddess touched a finger to his forehead, filling his body with energy. "Then rise as a guardian of the light and know that the future of all of Promethia rests upon your shoulders."

"No pressure," Cassie grumbled from behind him.

The goddess ignored the spitfire of a tank and kept her eyes focused on Tim's. "The Dark Lord's wraiths have already infiltrated the city. The sheriff might not be the only one. Find them and end them as you have done here."

Quest Received: Get the Wraiths Out of Here

The Dark Lord Vitaria has decided that now is the right time to conquer the city of Promethia. One of her wraiths has already been unmasked. You are charged with the task of finding the remaining wraiths and exterminating them.

Reward: Staff of Divine Retribution and five gold for each member of your party.

Accept Quest: Yes/No

Tim quickly accepted the quest.

The goddess smiled down upon their group as she started floating into the sky. "Paul will be able to provide you the answers you seek. The future of Promethia rests in your hands. Do not fail me, soldier of light." The goddess turned into a glowing ball and launched into the heavens.

Just like that, she was gone.

"She really does know how to make an exit," ShadowLily said, looking into the sky.

"That's the truth," JaKobi chimed in. "So, what do we do now?"

Tim grinned as he thought about the quests he had to turn in and how they should be enough to push him above level ten. "I've got a few quests to finish, but I'll meet everyone back at the inn and we'll figure out what to do about the goddess' quest."

"Sounds good to me." Cassie slung her bō staff into the holder on her back. "I need a beer after being in my own episode of *The Strain*." She shrugged. "Fighting face-sucking monsters isn't all it's cracked up to be."

"I second the beer comment but am reserving judgment on the monsters. I love a good horror flick." JaKobi grinned. "I mean, who doesn't want to save the world from monsters?"

Gaston raised his hand. "I just want a quiet life. A place where I can drink beer in peace."

Cassie smashed her elbow into Gaston's ribs. "I'm not buying that shit for one second." She smiled at the assassin's wounded expression. "Don't be such a baby. The first round's on me."

Gaston's mood brightened substantially. "Now you're speaking my language."

JaKobi gave Tim and ShadowLily a wave. "See you guys later." He shook his head as he turned away. "I swear, these guys run into the craziest shit," the fire mage mumbled. "I fucking love it."

Tim looked at the woman of his dreams as the guards started coming back into the space to see what happened. "You should go with them. I don't know how long this is going to take."

"Not a chance," ShadowLily smirked. "Last time I left you alone, you ended up in prison."

"At least you know I can satisfy your bad-boy craving," Tim responded with a flirty grin.

"The only thing you're bad at is staying out of jail," ShadowLily ribbed him.

Tim's grin got even bigger. "I'm going to take that as a compliment."

ShadowLily slapped him on the arm. "Not everything I say is a sex thing."

He couldn't stop himself from laughing but he gazed pleadingly into her eyes. "How about this one time? You gotta let me have this one."

"Fine." She put her hands on her hips and glared at him. "Sex was included in my previous statement, but it's not much of a compliment. I only said you weren't bad at it, not that you were great."

"But I *am* great, right?" Tim needled as they kept walking.

"Well, you're pretty good," she agreed reluctantly.

"A win's a win," Tim grinned from ear to ear. "Speaking of winning, as soon as we wrap this up, maybe we could do that one thing?"

"You want me to put on the pants I wore to the Stiff Tart again, don't you?" ShadowLily shook her head in mock disdain.

Tim only smirked at her. "See, you get me." Tim wrapped an arm around her as they headed toward the temple. "That's why we're perfect for each other."

ShadowLily paused and turned so she was looking directly into his eyes. "You really think so?"

"I do."

"Me too." She gave him a quick kiss and started pulling him toward the temple. "Let's get this over with. I've got a hot date and some tight pants to wriggle into."

"I'll do my best to make it quick." It was all Tim could do to not start running toward the temple. Getting back to the inn was now his highest priority.

CHAPTER TWENTY-FIVE

Now that he was out of combat, Tim's notifications were going crazy.

He pulled ShadowLily to a stop as they entered the temple. "Let me take care of a few things before we see Paul."

She nodded her head and started pulling up her own notifications. "Just let me know when you're done."

"Will do," Tim replied as he started looking over the data.

He'd almost hit level nine and still had a few quests to turn in. He'd be level ten by the end of the day for sure. A smile spread across Tim's lips as he thought about his team's future. They were almost at the point where things were really going to take off. The future was looking bright.

Tim pulled up his first notification.

Quest Completed: Something Wicked This Way Comes

You have discovered what was plaguing the prisoners and put an end to it. Not all of the prisoners survived, but at least the immediate threat has been curtailed.

Reward: Three gold coins

He'd give every one of those coins back to have Baron and Henry alive again. Tim would have wished them back to life for the simple fact that he wouldn't have to deliver their letters. It was one thing to know you were responsible for someone's death, and another thing entirely to have to explain your failure to their loved ones. Not that he had a choice now.

Those letters would get delivered.

No matter how much it hurt, it was his duty to get the last words of the sheriff's victims to their family members. So Tim would do it, and after stepping away from the situation for a few days, he'd re-examine every last bit of what happened to make sure those same mistakes were never repeated.

Maybe there wasn't anything he could have done. It wasn't like he could have stayed in jail, not with Lady Briarthorn outside demanding his release. Knowing their deaths were not his fault didn't make him feel any less guilty or the two men any less dead.

Without his new spells, Tim knew he wouldn't have been able to stop Jon Hobbs. The man had survived being immolated by JaKobi and having his chest filled with knives. Alone in the dark and without his new spells, Tim wouldn't have stood a chance.

There was a part of him that would always feel guilty about what had happened to Baron and Henry. Maybe he could talk to the high priest about doing a monthly healing in the Hole. It wouldn't bring the two men back, but it would ease his guilt. There was something to be said for paying penance. It helped keep the wound fresh so you would never forget what you were fighting for.

In this case, all of Promethia was on the line. Baron and Henry had been the first casualties of war, and their sacrifices wouldn't be forgotten. He'd deliver the letters, and make sure their families knew what they'd done.

Tim brushed away the **You've Reached Level Nine** notification.

He would worry about assigning his stat points after talking to Paul. With all his notifications taken care of or minimized, Tim turned toward ShadowLily. It felt kind of weird coming out of a fight without leveling at least one skill.

"Probably because those new spells were already apprentice level," Tim mumbled to himself.

ShadowLily dismissed whatever she was looking at. "Did you say something?"

Tim smiled as he looked at the most beautiful woman in the world. He didn't feel like explaining his thoughts about the fight, so he tried to get them focused on the next task they had to complete. "Let's go."

Walking deeper into the temple, Tim found one of the boys to escort them to Paul's chambers. As they walked through the dark and winding passages, he thought about what had happened over the last few days. Things hadn't gone exactly as expected, but in the end, everything had worked out.

At least, everything he could control.

What he couldn't control were monsters sent here to feed off people. Tim wasn't even sure what the bastards did. Jon Hobbs certainly wasn't sucking the blood out of the men, so the sheriff must have been feeding off of their essence somehow. That was some scary shit.

Hobbs had looked just fine in the sunlight too.

Monsters not being able to walk around in daylight was the thing that normally saved humans' asses in supernatural situations. It was a huge advantage to only have to worry about being attacked during half the day, and it was an added bonus if sunlight killed the monsters.

The sheriff had stood in broad daylight without so much as a blemish, as did Baron and Henry. That meant these wraiths could be hiding anywhere. Hobbs had been one hungry bastard, though, so maybe the way to track these new monsters was by looking for victims of their feedings.

Finding the wraiths and eliminating them was a problem

for another day. Tim still had plenty of work left to do before he could move on to the next task. There was a conversation with the high priest to be had and two letters to deliver before he could focus on the goddess' new quest.

Not to mention a district to revitalize, his job at the forge, and the healing shack. Tim's dance card was pretty full without having to track and hunt the wraiths, but he'd find them. Once Promethia was secure, they could take the fight to Vitaria.

Their runner dropped them off outside of the high priest's chambers. Unlike every other trip Tim had made to visit the high priest, the large golden doors were open. With Jepsom out of the way, Paul seemed more confident in his security.

"The hero of the day returns." Paul clapped as he stood up and walked toward Tim. "Your ability to take control of the situation and save the day was very impressive."

Tim shook Paul's hand. "I was just doing my part."

"And humble. Most heroes are braggarts by nature. They seek out the jobs that will put them in the spotlight." Paul dropped Tim's hand and smiled warmly. "But not you. The goddess truly shines within you."

"I wouldn't go that far." Tim stopped when ShadowLily elbowed him in the ribs. "But her light does guide me."

"As it does for us all." Paul motioned for Tim to join him by the throne. The high priest started digging around in the chest behind his chair. "I believe a reward is in order."

Quest Complete: Wrath of the goddess

Cardinal Jepsom met his untimely end, and while it wasn't done by your hand, his death wouldn't have been possible without your influence on the events leading to the deed. You've also managed to stoke the embers of peoples' beliefs into righteous flames of faith for the goddess' salvation.

Reward: Fifty gold coins.

Paul smiled as he handed Tim the giant sack of coins. "I've

also restored your privileges in the temple and awarded you the rank of Honorary Brother. If ever you find yourself in need, the temple will always be a place of refuge."

"Thank you for doing your duty to the realm and the goddess. I am sure you have plenty of questions, but in the aftermath of the attack, I have a lot of work to do. If you need help with research or just general information, seek out Brother Colton in the library. If anyone can shed light on what's happening now, it's him."

Tim shook Paul's hand again. "Thank you." He paused after letting Paul's hand drop and quickly added. "Before I go, I wonder if you have the time to consider a simple request."

"If it's in my power to do it, it will be so." Paul's eyes bored into Tim with feverish intensity.

"Without the help of the two men Jon Hobbs murdered for his attack today, I wouldn't have made it out of the Hole. I was wondering if you could grant me some kind of special dispensation so I could heal the inmates once a month."

Tim looked at the floor, not sure why he was seeking validation for his idea and not just the approval to carry it out. "It would be a nice way to pay back the memory of two men who tried to do the right thing."

"This is why I like working with you." Paul beamed. "You are always coming up with new ways to spread the goddess' light. I will help you get the documents you need, and I would be honored to preside over the services of the two men."

"Thank you," Tim replied. He pulled Paul into a heartfelt hug. "Having their loved ones honored by the temple might bring their families some peace."

Paul waved away Tim's thanks. "It is the least I can do." He clapped his hands, and one of his personal guards stepped forward. "Please show them out."

"Right this way." The guard pointed toward the door and led Tim and ShadowLily out of the temple.

CHAPTER TWENTY-SIX

Completing Paul's quest had made Tim level ten.

All he had to do before becoming an adventurer was pick his advanced class, but there would be time for him to worry about that task after completing his last open quest. The delivery of his first letter to a very gruff and unimpressed Felix Hardgrove hadn't gone nearly as well as Tim would have liked.

Snatching the letter and slamming the door in Tim's face wasn't exactly warm and fuzzy.

While a warm and fuzzy response wasn't exactly what he'd been expecting, he was caught off-guard by the abruptness of the entire interaction. Given the news Tim had to deliver, he was willing to give Felix a pass. He didn't know how police and doctors could constantly deliver bad news to grieving families and not be broken. Tim had only done the deed once, and it was enough to make him want to crawl into bed for a week and live on a diet of ice cream and pizza.

Now they were halfway to Helen Peters' house, and Tim was preparing himself for a tough conversation. Maybe getting the Jehovah's Witness treatment earlier had been a blessing in disguise. At least he didn't have to explain himself and deal with the aftermath.

Nothing sucked the fun out of the room faster than a death.

Tim stopped at the edge of the path leading to a small cottage and pulled ShadowLily into a hug. "Thank you for staying with me."

"Are you sure you don't want me to come to the door?" the half-elf asked as she watched him with concern.

"I'll be fine." Tim scuffed his boots in the dirt. "I just have to pull off the Band-Aid."

ShadowLily spun him so he was facing the door. "Then do it."

It was just the kick in the pants Tim needed to get moving. He started walking up the well-maintained path toward the house. ShadowLily was hanging back by the gate, so he had the space to handle the delivery himself. The warm and fuzzy feeling he was getting right now was from the knowledge she'd be right there waiting for him no matter how things went.

Life was so much better when you had at least one person you could always count on.

Tim stopped in front of the door, his heart racing. There was really no good way to deliver bad news, and drawing it out only made it worse for everyone. So did lingering on someone's doorstep. No one liked it when a random stranger was hanging out in their front yard.

Taking a deep, calming breath, Tim knocked on the door.

A few minutes later, a plump middle-aged woman opened the door a crack. Peering out of the opening, she gave Tim a quick once-over. "Can I help you?"

Tim dug deep into his emotional toolbox and managed to generate a weak smile. "My name is Tim. I'm a friend of Baron's."

"There's a name I haven't heard in ages." Helen Peters

opened the door a bit wider. "What's that old rapscallion have to say for himself?"

The smile vanished from Tim's face. "I hate to be the one to have to tell you this." He took his eyes off of hers and looked at the ground. "He's dead."

Helen looked shaken but not taken off-guard. "You know, I always thought I'd see him again."

"I was with him the day before he passed. He gave me a letter." Tim fished the letter out of his cloak and handed it to her. "I'm not sure what kind of life Baron led before I met him, but he was a friend to me when I needed one, and he died fighting for the people of Promethia."

"That doesn't sound much like the Baron I knew." Helen eyed him suspiciously.

Tim wasn't sure what to say. His brain defaulted to sarcastic whenever he was nervous or in trouble. His mouth opened, and the words came tumbling out. "Well, he *was* in prison at the time."

Oh, shit! Here he was delivering a death notification, and now he was cracking fucking jokes. Was he the worst person in the world?

"That sounds more like him." Helen slapped her thigh as she laughed. She looked up, the glimmer of a memory lighting her gaze. "But you say he died doing something good?"

"He died trying to save all of us from a threat. The high priest is going to preside over his services." Tim smiled warmly. "No matter his faults, in the end, he was a good man."

Tears streaked Helen's cheeks. "That he was, young man, that he was." She clutched the letter to her chest. "Thank you for coming to tell me."

Tim gave her a little bow. "It was my pleasure to do this for him. If you ever need anything, you can find me at the Blue Dagger Inn."

"That place in the slums?" Helen questioned.

"The very one." Tim laughed. "It might not seem like much yet, but we're working on it."

Helen patted him gently on the arm. "I doubt I'll need anything, but if I do, I promise to call on you." She gave him one last smile and went inside to read the note.

Tim turned and walked back down the path. He felt lighter than he had when they reached Helen's home. She seemed like such a sweet lady. Tim wondered if Baron had gone off to make his fortune only to never return. There was a story there somewhere, but it wasn't the right time to ask.

ShadowLily wrapped an arm around him as he drew closer. "That seemed to go well."

"It did. I get the feeling they hadn't talked in a while, but it was one of those relationships that no matter how long it had been since they saw each other, it was as if only a few minutes had passed." Tim pulled ShadowLily against him. "It might sound sappy, but I don't know what I'd do if you just disappeared and I had no way to find you."

"I'd burn down the world to find you?" ShadowLily said with a hint of anger in her voice. It was the kind of tone that implied anyone who fucked with her man better get the hell out of dodge, and quickly.

Tim laughed. "Maybe start with something a little more subtle."

"Said no one ever." She stopped him and looked into Tim's eyes. "Haven't you seen *Taken*, you've got to be on top of this shit before it's too late."

"The next part is very important. They are going to take you," Tim intoned in his best Liam Neeson impression. "I like to replace the word *take* with *tickle*, though."

ShadowLily started to sprint away from him. "Oh, no, you don't."

"The next part is very important," Tim yelled as he chased after her. "I am going to tickle you and there is nothing you can do about it." He held his hands up fingers extended. The digits twitched slightly in anticipation of touching woman-flesh.

"Buahahahahaha!" Tim roared as he started chasing her toward the inn. He might not get her now, but eventually, she'd let her guard down, and the tickling would begin.

EPILOGUE

Mornings sucked.

Seriously, was there ever a good time for it to be morning? Tim thought as he rolled out of bed. The only time anyone looked forward to mornings was if there was a new release of some kind. Otherwise, the world would like to sleep in until a respectable hour.

Tim looked at the empty half of the bed and realized that maybe he just wasn't a morning person. Was enjoying mornings a conscious decision? Could he wake up one day and just attack the day like one of "those people?"

He took his first lumbering steps toward the door and smelled the coffee waiting for him on the other side. Liz was an amazing person. Tim would sing her praises until the end of time for always knowing when he was going to wake up and having that sweet dark cup of roasted delight ready.

He'd heard tea drinkers refer to coffee as bean water. If that were the case, they were just drinking tree leaves. Those snobby bastards didn't even have the sense to brew them properly. There was a whole art to crafting the perfect cup of coffee.

Tim's personal setup looked like a science experiment gone wrong, but the product was divine.

Oddly enough, he wasn't opposed to a good cup of tea. Tim never claimed to be coffee-exclusive, not unless it was the first drink of the day. Sure, a good dark tea had some pick-me-up, but nothing rocked the house like a cup of joe with a shot of his second-favorite bean for an extra jolt. Expresso was like the kicker on a football team. He was important. You couldn't win without him, but most of the time, he just rode the bench.

He wasn't even sure if they had expresso here, but it took him about five minutes of explaining for Liz to figure out what he wanted and find it. The woman was like a wizard when it came to anticipating their needs. The coffee waiting outside of his door in the morning was just one example.

Tim never realized how important it was to get the first cup of coffee down on the way to the bathroom. He'd always been a set the coffee maker and get dressed kind of guy. Then it was coffee for breakfast as he ran out the door. Not at the Blue Dagger.

He had his first cup down before he sat down to take his morning sabbatical.

By the time Tim climbed into his bath, the coffee almost made him feel like a human being again. He hated to admit it, but he might be slightly jealous of the get-up-and-go types. His bed might as well have been his sanctuary. He only wanted to leave it when absolutely necessary.

That meant his relationship, food, work, and raiding were the only things standing between him and the sleep he craved.

Even now that his work was going to be kicking ass full-time, there still wouldn't be enough hours in the day for napping. Four hours a day at the forge, and another four in the healing shack, plus a nightly run of some kind with the group was leaving him a little ragged.

Maybe it was just that he hadn't settled on a new class yet?

There were so many good options. Did he want to push on as a straight healer, or did he want to be a little more adventurous? It had been a few days since Jepsom died, and his life hadn't slowed down one bit.

He'd settle on a class before he had the meeting with his caseworker. Apparently, becoming an adventurer meant he had to pause his life in-game to sign a new contract. At least he'd be able to set up access to the currency market.

From the marketplace, he could sell his gold to people for real-world currency, and from there, it was a few simple steps to get that money to his parents. He'd feel a lot better telling his parents about his decision after he sent them some money. Nothing made your choices look better than success.

There was so much to do, and he was just getting started. His project in the slums was underway, with Mr. Applebottom overseeing the details. A few of the buildings would be ready by the end of the month.

That meant it was time to put his market kiosk into play. Once people started coming for the market, it would be easier to get the prices he wanted for rent on the newly refurbished structures.

With renters in place and his percentage from the kiosk, getting more gold should never be a problem. He leaned back, letting the warm water ease the tension in his muscles. He loved the thirty minutes he took for himself every morning. It was the only time he got to let his mind wander.

A buzz sounded in Tim's head and pulled him right out of the tranquility zone.

Could people not wait until a decent hour to contact him? And why the fuck had the message buzzed through his filters? Tim sighed in frustration as he pulled up his user interface. The first thing he saw was a reminder to pick his class. Dismissing the window, Tim moved onto his messages. He had a priority message from Jeremy.

Wow, he hadn't seen Jeremy since his first day in the game. Not since the man had pointed him toward the inn and said something funny to him. What was it his guide had said? The words didn't immediately come back to him, so he decided to open his new message and find out what he wanted.

Message Received From Jeremy:
I've got someone who wants to meet you. See you in five. Eat a Fish!

"What does that even mean?" Tim closed the message and climbed out of the bath. Regardless of the daring it took to try to come up with a cool new catchphrase, he wasn't sure "eat a fish" was ever going to catch on. Sure, maybe if you ran a fish taco truck and needed a cool slogan, but otherwise, it just seemed kinda weird.

Despite the friendly feel of Jeremy's message, Tim wondered if he was doing another job for NPC Corp. If the man was working for the company, it wouldn't pay to keep him waiting. He finished drying off and equipped his clothes.

Getting dressed in an instant was never going to get old.

Walking into the main room of the inn, Tim motioned toward his cup and then at Liz. She nodded, and he set it on the counter before heading to the door. He had to admit that living at the inn had its perks.

Tim opened the front door and stepped onto the street before he stretched his back. Jeremy was leading a man he'd never seen before toward him. Part of Tim was jealous that he'd never be able to rock an afro the way Jeremy did. The man had a certain 70s funk about him that was cool as fuck and definitely couldn't be replicated.

The man walking next to Jeremy was about forty. He had a wide, solid-looking frame, and his arms rippled with thickly corded muscles. The guy had on the same starting tunic Tim had been given when he entered the game. Maybe it was the man's first day in Promethia. It was kind of awesome that new people were starting to play every day. The more popular the game was, the easier it would be to make money.

The two men joined him on the porch. Jeremey pointed to the man next to him. "This is Joe. Joe, this is Tim." Jeremy gave Joe's hand a brief shake. "Good luck to you." He turned and headed back the way he'd come.

Tearing his gaze from Jeremy, Tim looked at the man in front of him, wondering what this was about. Something about his face looked incredibly familiar, but he couldn't place it.

Joe stuck out his hand. "It's good to see you again, Tim. I trust you've been taking good care of my daughter."

Holy shit!

It was *that* Joe. Sierra's dad was in the game, and he was here right now. They hadn't discussed what they would tell their parents about their relationship. It just seemed too weird. How did you say, "Hey, Dad, we fell in love in a videogame, and we will be making a life for ourselves here. It's cool, trust me."

Thoughts of what would happen if Joe found out they were basically living together rattled around inside his head loud enough that it took him a few moments to respond. "It's good to see you too, sir. Sierra is in good hands with me." It was overly formal, but he found it was always best to be exceedingly polite in situations where he was terrified.

Sierra's dad wasn't a gamer, he was a cook. What was he doing here?

"Good to hear." He clapped Tim on the shoulder. "Anywhere we can talk in private for a minute?"

Tim wasn't sure how private Joe wanted their conversation to be. He'd obviously come to Tim before Sierra, so something was up, but he had no idea what the man wanted. He hoped it wouldn't be a morning lecture about sex before marriage. Then there was Sierra to think about. She was probably inside training with Gaston, so taking Joe into the inn was out.

That left one place for him to go.

"Follow me." Tim waved to Joe as he set off around the side of the building. He opened the shack and motioned for Joe to join him. Once they were both inside, he closed the door and waited for his unexpected guest to say something.

Joe looked at him for a moment, and then in a rush, he blurted, "I sold my restaurant."

"What?" Tim was shocked. Joe's was an institution. The fucking diner should be a landmark, not something that was bought or sold.

"I couldn't bear the thought of my girl growing up in here and missing all those memories. I don't care where we spend our time together as a family. Being with one another is all that matters." Joe looked at Tim. "I just don't know how to tell her."

Tim was still trying to play catch up. "Wait, you sold your restaurant?"

"Yeah." Joe looked a little bummed about it. "Got a hell of a price from some corporate assholes who wanted the location for some crappy chain." He shrugged. "Thought I could open a restaurant in the game. Things can't be too different."

"You're going to need someone to help you adjust. Some of the things here have different names." Tim smiled sheepishly. "Although you could always just go to the market and point at the things you want."

"Should be fun?" He leaned forward, looking a little worried. "First, I'm going to need some new clothes." Joe's face turned almost ashen. "Do NPCs even eat?"

This was one thing Tim could answer easily. "They sure do, and they like to drink." He started to get excited about the idea. "But I'm also sure there are plenty of people here who would kill for a taste of home."

"I'm counting on it." Joe wrung his hands. "Feeding people is what I like to do. All I have to do now is find a place and set up shop."

"Just so happens I might be able to help you with that, but

first, we need to let ShadowLily know you're here." Tim put a hand on Joe's shoulder. "And get you some clothes. I can't have my girlfriend's dad showing up in a smock."

"Ah, so it's 'girlfriend' now." Joe watched Tim intently.

"Yes, sir."

Joe let Tim suffer for a few more seconds before he started to laugh. "I'm pretty sure I called it before you left."

Tim just nodded. It was funny how parents could see things before their kids did. It must come with experience.

"What I'd really like to do is cook her favorite meal for her." Joe smiled as he thought about it. "God knows, she can't go a week without eating a plate of chicken parm."

Chicken-fucking-parmesan!

"How would you feel about cooking enough for a group?" Tim started thinking about how much the entire guild would appreciate a real meal, especially after weeks of stew.

He paused when he realized he was trying to hijack Joe's moment with his daughter. He held up a hand to stop Joe before he could answer. "Sorry, it was a stupid idea. This moment is about you and Sierra."

"You remember she was in the restaurant before she left with a booth full of her friends? I wouldn't mind cooking for a few of her new ones. Not to mention, it's really just as easy to cook for twenty as it is for two." Joe smiled. "As long as you have a kitchen I can use."

Tim had access to a kitchen, all right. "Let me go and set things up with Ernie. Then I'll find ShadowLily and take her out until tonight. We'll come back to the inn, and you can lay it on her."

"That sounds like a good plan, but why is she here? Doesn't she have her own place?" Joe watched Tim like a dog eyeing a stray burger at a barbeque.

"You'll have to ask her that tonight." Tim opened the door,

prepared to run. "Give me about fifteen minutes before you head inside."

Joe nodded, keeping his steely gaze focused on Tim.

Secrets weren't his strong suit, but Tim would have to try his best. His hand closed on the door to the inn, and he smiled. "I've got this."

"Today was such a blast." ShadowLily grinned as she yanked Tim toward the inn. "But I'm hungry. Why couldn't we stop and get something to eat?" the half-elf questioned as she picked up her pace.

"I told you, we've got a guild dinner tonight. If you don't like the food, don't eat anything, and we'll go out afterward." Tim grinned. "Or I could order some of those little cakes you like."

"Petit fours." She stopped walking, savoring the thought of her favorite mini-cake snack. "I can sit through anything for a box of those sweet, sweet delights."

"Good to know for when I have to ask you to do something you don't like." Tim pulled out an imaginary pen and paper to take a note.

"Just promise me it isn't stew. Liz picked the cook already. By now, he should be able to make more stuff." ShadowLily sighed. "I never knew how good I had it, being able to eat at my dad's restaurant."

Tim grinned as he pushed her toward the door. "I made Liz promise we would have something else tonight."

"That's sexy talk." ShadowLily pushed open the door to the inn and paused in her tracks. "What's that heavenly smell?"

She spun. "It smells just like home." She gave him an accusatory glare. "What'd you do?"

"He didn't do anything." Joe came out of the kitchen, wiping his hands on an apron.

"Dad?" ShadowLily paused for a second as she let his presence register. Once she realized it was really him, she rushed forward and pulled him into a hug. "What are you doing here?"

Joe hugged her back and took a step back so he could give her a solid once-over. "Changed your ears," he mumbled before returning his gaze to her eyes. "I sold my place. Couldn't bear the thought of being away from you for so long."

ShadowLily started to grin. "And what's that I smell?"

"Only your favorite," Joe replied swiftly.

Tim motioned for everyone to head to the tables. "Tonight, we feast like gods!"

"Hear, hear," the room shouted back.

Tim looked at their growing band and couldn't have been happier. It was nice that Sierra and Joe were going to get to spend more time together. Ok, so maybe he was more excited about the food possibilities that had just come back into his life, but you could be happy for more than one reason at a time, right?

Things were starting to come together in the best possible way. They had a new quest to look forward to and new monsters to hunt. *The Etheric Coast* was just as fresh today as the first instant he stepped into the game. He took a drink of his ale and smiled. Tim wasn't sure what would happen next, but he knew they'd be ready for it.

The Blue Dagger Society was ready for anything.

List of Tim's Current Stats and Skills.

"Tim" Level ten magic user

. . .

Primary Stats
    Strength 12
    Endurance 12
    Dexterity 16
    Intelligence 16
    Wisdom 30
    Perception: 5
    Vitality: 3
    Revitalization: 3
    Luck: 5

Tim also has two undistributed stat points.

Notable Gear
    Circlet of Wisdom +1
    Simple Dagger of Dexterity +1 (X2)
    Level Ten Class Change Token
    Boots of Wisdom +2
    Robe of the Everlasting: Wisdom +3
    Belt of Wisdom +2
    Gloves of Wisdom +2

Skills
    Healing Orb: Apprentice rank nine
    Dodge: Novice rank two
    Flame Burst: Apprentice rank three
    Cleanse: Apprentice rank seven
    Appeal to the Goddess: Novice rank one
    Infiltrator: Novice rank three

Small Blades: Apprentice rank six
Throwing Knives: Apprentice rank two
Sneak: Apprentice rank three
Night Vision: Novice rank five
Back Stab: Novice rank seven
Weaken Undead: Apprentice rank one
Divine Light: Apprentice rank one
Healing Storm: Novice level one

Open Quests
Get the Wraith Out of Here

LOOKING FOR DPS

The story continues with book four, LOOKING FOR DPS, coming soon to Amazon and Kindle Unlimited.

BOOKS BY BRADFORD BATES

Ascendancy Legacy
The Arena

Jar of Souls

Guardian of the Grove

Demon Stone

The Rising Darkness

Redemption

Ascendancy Origins
Rise of the Fallen

Butcher of the Bay

Night of the Demon

The Bozley Green Chronicles
Possessed

The Galactic Outlaws
Forced Compliance

Genetic Purge

Smuggler's Legacy

Fortune Hunters
Star Talon

Lost Signal

A Galactic Outlaws Story

The Marchenko Incident

Smuggler for Hire

Origin Ice

The Fairy of Salem

Witching Hour

The Wild Hunt

Standalone Titles

Crimson Stars

BOOKS BY MICHAEL ANDERLE

Sign up for the LMBPN email list to be notified of new releases and special deals!

https://lmbpn.com/email/

For a complete list of books by Michael Anderle, please visit:

www.lmbpn.com/ma-books/

CONNECT WITH THE AUTHORS

Connect with Bradford Bates

Facebook:
https://www.facebook.com/bradfordbatesauthor/

Twitter:
https://twitter.com/Freetheblizz

Website:
http://www.bradfordbates.com/

Connect with Michael Anderle and sign up for his email list here:

Website: http://lmbpn.com

Email List: https://michael.beehiiv.com/

https://www.facebook.com/LMBPNPublishing

https://twitter.com/MichaelAnderle

https://www.instagram.com/lmbpn_publishing/

https://www.bookbub.com/authors/michael-anderle

ABOUT BRADFORD BATES

Bradford Bates is a full-time author, husband to an incredible wife, and father to four furry rescue dogs. He lives in sunny Phoenix, Arizona, trying to not melt in the oppressive heat of the summer. When he isn't busy writing the next book, you can find him playing video games and watching scary movies.

www.ingramcontent.com/pod-product-compliance
Lightning Source LLC
LaVergne TN
LVHW041801060526
838201LV00046B/1075